Hindi Short Stories

Editor's Choice

Selected & Translated by
Girdhar Rathi

THORNBIRD
NIYOGI BOOKS

Published by
NIYOGI BOOKS
Block D, Building No. 77,
Okhla Industrial Area, Phase-I,
New Delhi-110 020, INDIA
Tel: 91-11-26816301, 26818960
Email: niyogibooks@gmail.com
Website: www.niyogibooksindia.com

Editor: Arunima Ghosh
Design: Nabanita Das

ISBN: 978-93-86906-61-8
Publication: 2018

Printed at: Niyogi Offset Pvt. Ltd., New Delhi, India

Contents

Translator's Note

A Long Decade

Presented here is a selection of 17 short stories, broadly from the 1960s—a 'long decade' that unfurled its wings a little before 1960, and cast its shadow over the early years of the 1970s (a highly eventful decade in the unfolding of the history of Independent India). For Hindi literature, it was a remarkable time of resurgence. Magazines like *Kriti, Kalpana, Kahani* and then *Nayi Kahaniyan, Dharmayuga, Saptahik Hindustan,* and later on *Dinman,* etc. were enticingly enlarging the literary and artistic readership; and at the same time providing the platform for the works of renowned and budding talents. Several cities and towns were competing among themselves to claim the first place in producing and displaying their creative wares—as far apart as Patna, Lucknow, Allahabad, Delhi, Kolkata and Hyderabad! (Later on, alas! Everything got confined to Delhi—all our provincial power houses foreclosed, just like the great breeding grounds of Indian Coffee Houses!)

It was a decade full of wars, strife, drought and famine. Perhaps the fiercest battle then being fought was over languages: a battle against the evident dominance of English, and apparent predominance of Hindi, for Hindi and all Indian languages, and even for English! In the process, most of our languages brought forth some of their finest and (now) classic works! And not only in literature. Also in films, music, theatre, dance, etc.

Even though battling for primacy in the pecking order, the languages were embracing each other: Dharmveer Bharti, Vijay Tendulkar, Girish

Karnad, Badal Sircar and numerous other names became the darlings of theatre-lovers all over the country. So also other names in other genres.

Just to reassure myself, I went out interviewing people like Bhanu Bharti, Suraj Ghai, K.G. Verma, Ravindra Verma, Prayag Shukla and others. There also appeared a series of interviews in a newspaper further fortifying my hunch. These notes need another volume! And yet I felt a little unsure.

As if to buttress the dwindling confidence in my own overview of the 'long decade', I jumped at this piece in the *Hindu Literary Magazine* (7 January 2018) about a great Tamil writer: When 44 Dalits were killed by a landlord in Keezhvenmani in 1968, Indira Parthasarathy was compelled to visit the place and write on it, 'These days, they happen all over—atrocities against Dalits. And nobody seems shocked. Back then, we were really shocked. I somehow wanted to write on it... Because I firmly believe writing is a social act. Any art work for that matter.'

Though torn between hope and hopelessness, the various generations active in those years did produce some changes for the better, even if the changes did not last too long. On the global scale, for example, voices (though admittedly not just literary voices) against the American war in Vietnam did seem to make some difference. In India, the monolith of Congress Party rule was cracked, even broken. Great splits took place in ideologies, intellectual and academic paradigms, in political parties. The scope for free thinking and free expression thus did widen. Democracy, universalism, non-obscurantism, liberalism and secularism were words that seemed to carry a lot of conviction and value. There was, decidedly, less cynicism, much less careerism, hardly any 'terrorism'—despite the Naxalite emergence. Youth power in Euro-America as well as in India, came to be reckoned with for the first time. At its birth, Youth Power was highly idealistic. These stories were translated in Tihar (Delhi) and

Jaipur jails—during the Internal Emergency imposed on 25–26 June 1975. Soon after, they were published in various magazines, newspapers, and some in anthologies in India and abroad. It was only in 2004 that I submitted the bunch to Mrs Chandra Chari, the redoubtable editor of *The Book Review*. The very next morning I was thrilled to hear her phone me to say that it was a *dharohar* (treasure trove), and that she would like to publish and release the book in the London Book Fair. What was the USP of this selection, she asked. I was hard put to answer that. These were the works of some of my favourite authors. I knew them personally, and the only criterion was that I had liked these stories!

And then an entire era came alive for me. It was a 'long decade'. It began unfurling its wings a little before 1960, and continued to cast its shadow. In a sense, my generation is a creature of this period. Someday, someone will surely dig deep into the history of this era.

However, I could not produce an introduction to the collection though the stories had been typeset and even proofread! It was a peculiar writer's block! I apologize to Mrs Chari. I thank her and Geeta Parameswaram for preserving and graciously offering the typescript even after so many years.

And I owe it to my dear friend, Nirmalkanti Bhattacharjee, that finally the selection is available in book form, published by Niyogi Books. All the stories here, in fact, were widely acclaimed in the original. Should a reader, however, feel cheated in any way, the blame must be directed to me, the translator.

Girdhar Rathi

Introduction

Deep down it is possible to fish out some theme—say, privation, though of several kinds—common to all these 17 stories. But the nine writers selected here have their own very distinct voices, none overlapping or imitating any other. This is a limited way that may be considered as a sampling of the myriad colours the modern Hindi (short) fiction offers.

English-reading connoisseurs are likely to be more familiar with Nirmal Verma whose major works are available in translation. He had sort of heralded the Nayi Kahani (New Story) movement in the 1950's with his first collection: *Parinde* (*Hill Station and Other Stories*). But Nirmal Verma stood almost alone among the co-pioneers (Mohan Rakesh, Kamaleshwar, Rajendra Yadav and others) with his light-and-shade play of language, reflective and self-reflexive mode of narration, metaphorical and imagistic composition, and sonorous yet disturbing voice.

Prague Spring (1968) brought for him the end of his decade-long stay in Czechoslovakia and romance with Marxism, where he translated some great Czech writers into Hindi, long before their worldwide fame.

Nirmal Verma's engagement with existential angst over the human condition and destiny is manifest in his novels, essays, diaries, travelogues and short stories. He had emerged as a fine cultural critic and literary theorist, confronting the worldviews of the West and the East, modernism and postmodernism, questions of civilizational crises and so on. 'The World Elsewhere' can be seen as the culmination of his specific search and style, a world, eerie and unreal, yet so very real to the little girl, living with her lonely mother, a West-Indian in London. And 'A Night in

London' is an understated yet horrifying depiction of an 'omnipresent' racism. Exile, alienation, unfulfilled youthful yearnings, impotent rage against the colonial degradation—all these make it a multi-layered masterpiece.

Ram Kumar, his elder brother had started writing stories in the 1940's, though outside the Hindi literary world he is known more for his paintings. So far eight collections of short stories, two novels, and a travelogue, apart from his pieces on art, an interview with George Lukais and Mrs Romain Rolland etc., are highly valued by readers. In English, *Ram Kumar: The Face & Other Stories* (Vadehra Art Gallery, New Delhi) offers some ten stories and a few drawings of his.

As Prayag Shukla puts it: 'In Ram Kumar's stories there is no drama or melodrama and there are no unusual turn of events either, in the lives of the characters. Instead, there are meditative moods... fine descriptions of locales and seasons, especially summers... Memory plays a very definitive role. ...In every story of his, there is a strange juxtaposition of "sound and silence".'

His concerns and vision pervade both his writings and paintings, though they do not 'illustrate' each other. His sad, brooding youths, scenes of Benaras (Varanasi) full of dark mystique, and later on his fascinating abstracts with layers within layers, have sometimes reversed the conventional significations of colours. Even a vibrant red can be sad, he once said (Amrita Shergil, the Hungarian-Indian painter, too, had seen and shown the sad red in her paintings). It is one of his abstract paintings that has been used for the cover of this book.

In Raghuvir Sahay, the Hindi modern short story gains from the wit of a seasoned journalist and the wisdom of a major poet. Like Kunwar Narain, Shrikant Verma, Vinod Kumar Shukla, Prayag Shukla etc., he is one of the poet-fictionists who gave a 'truly new kind of story' in the heydays of 'Nayi Kahani' movement—as Vijay Mohan Singh averred while writing about his 'Sathottari' generation (post-1960s).

Raghuvir Sahay was a creative mind who never rested on his laurels. Constantly trying to grasp 'the society that we are building,' he has touched, in his short stories too, extreme ends: from sheer absurd and abstract to most concrete and rational. Irony, self-deprecation, sarcasm, satire, mockery—every kind of weapon in the arsenal of a social commentator is used in abundance—only to underwrite the unwavering compassion innate in humanism.

As a journalist too, as the editor of the weekly *Dinman*, he mentored scores of young men and women who are now respected journalists and writers. His passion to bring poetry to people made him set poetry to music, and dramatize and stage it. His stage versions of Shakespeare, and his translation of fiction and poetry from Hungary and Poland have set their own standards.

Mahendra Bhalla, his later days were popular in Delhi theatre circles with his plays, and he had taken to poetry in a big way. Sparing and bore in language but unsparing in his attack on sham and self-delusions, his poetry stood apart from his plays; his dramas were forcefully articulate.

But 'Ek Pati Ke Notes' (Notes of a Husband) seems to have become a perennial favourite of the readers. This was the story with which he had stormed the scene in the 1960s. Mahendra Bhalla had evolved a fictional diction which was stark, direct, unsentimental and hard-hitting. He had grappled with the overwhelming realities of the emergent independent nation, which included sloth, envy, dirt, deprivations and crumbling moral structures. His long sojourn in England also gave us a trilogy of novels that unveiled the racial indignities suffered by Indians.

He can be counted among the post-colonial pioneers who for the first time began to detail the sufferings of Indian immigrants—

and the transformation they underwent. Motherland, after that experience of creature comforts (and despite moral degradation), looked alienating to them. Mahendra Bhalla was fond of saying: We have ugliness all around us, because we don't love 'life'. 'Doggery', presented here, was a hot topic on its first publication, among the literary community.

Compared to other 'sathottari' (post-1960s) writers, Ram Narayan Shukla would use the language in a 'functional' way: Even when deploying symbolism, he would render feelings, arguments, dialogues in a straight manner. Read between the lines, this prose gave a complex resonance. Simplicity itself became haunting.

In a sense, Ram Narayan Shukla was amongst the most realistic in his style, and yet the brooding, melancholic, understated, non-aggressive and non-vehement stance very often evokes his comparison with Ram Kumar.

In his very short life, he had penned more than 60 stories, collected in three volumes apart from two anthologies. He also translated from Bengali and English, and helped edit *Kahani*, the monthly that played a crucial role in the 'Nayi Kahani' movement.

Ram Narayan Shukla and Gyan Prakash were close friends, and their styles are totally different. In the several collections and two novels, Gyan Prakash applied bitter satire to delineate the inequities and absurdities of day to day existence of the middle classes. Corruption in the system and the corrosion of the human soul could be said to be his leitmotif. There is a peculiar streak of humour in his sobering narration.

Working throughout in a constricting environment of a government office, he had participated in the employees' struggles and had suffered imprisonment, too. In his last days, I shudder as I recall, he lived almost like an 'Aghori' with his loving, grown up children—perhaps devout and yet completely cynical to the worldly ways. Life, here, seemed to imitate his art.

Gyan Ranjan is regarded as one of the tallest figures in the post-1960s group. *Pita* (Father), *Fence Ke Idhar aur Udhar* (On Either Side of the Fence) and several other collections of stories, a novel, and an autobiographical account of his are proof enough of a very powerful, innovative creativity. The very edge of his sharp, acerbic, lashing tongue alerts you to a new idiom.

For the first time, generational gap seemed to have come into focus with Gyan Ranjan. Snobbery, cant, sham—so very evident in relationships and social environs at large made him—and his readers—quite impatient. It is also tempting to compare his 'Flunkey' with Mahendra Bhalla's 'Doggery'. The class division in 'Flunkey' is rather firmly etched out; it is also more concerned with the culture-vultures in a capitalist order of things. 'Doggery', on the other hand, seems to drag down the haves towards the community of have-nots, in a hopelessly decadent system. The last few decades have seen Gyan Ranjan engaged in editing *Pahal,* a journal that has instantiated him from the creative fiction.

Govind Mishra, too, encompasses a vast territory of social and personal experiences. *Lal Peeli Zamin* (Red-yellow Ground), his novel had massively attracted the attention of critics, who were already appreciative of his style of short fiction. With several novels, collections of short stories, essays and interviews to his credit, Govind Mishra has also dealt with the uneven terrains presented by the social milieu to the less privileged. More often than not, he leaves the statements or observations half-articulated. In a way, this invites the reader to participate, to try and complete the utterance. In some of his works, one can see several generations, and several different historical-cultural periods come alive. Literature is truly his obsession; for it, he was quite often willing to give up cushier positions of power.

Prayag Shukla happens to be the younger brother of Ram Narayan Shukla. Aged around 18, he had already attracted the attention of some major writers and editors with his short stories. Apparently, 'A Friend in the Street' is his first published story. Today, he is very well known as an art critic and curator of several art exhibitions in India and abroad. He is a very popular writer among children. A highly regarded poet, who has shunned the ever-changing literary fashions, and has concentrated on the finer stirrings of heart and soul.

As a professional literary journalist, he began his journey with the iconic *Kalpana* magazine, and went on to become the founding editor of several other journals, working also with *Dinman*, etc.

His short stories, novels, travelogues, memoirs and translations of Bengali and international poets—including Tagore, Shakh Ghosh and Octaviopaz—and many other publications undergird an untiring creativity. Soft-spoken, his gaze sees through things and people and situations. Brooding, but not overtly gloomy. Knots of everyday problems, difficulties, dilemmas; knots of memory; a painterly eye for details; a nuanced and balanced turn of phrase: Prayag Shukla is recognizable in this way.

Girdhar Rathi

Ram Kumar

Ram Kumar (1924–2018) has been acclaimed as one of India's foremost painters. He was associated with the Progressive artists' group along with M.F. Hussain, Tyeb Mehta, S.H. Raza. His works are rich with complex motifs, abstract cityscapes and landscapes, and unique among his immediate contemporaries. His short stories, novels, travelogues and essays are highly valued in the Hindi literary world for their innovative perspectives and novel sensibilities. In 1972, Padma Shri, and in 1985, Kalidas Samman are among the many decorations and awards he was conferred upon.

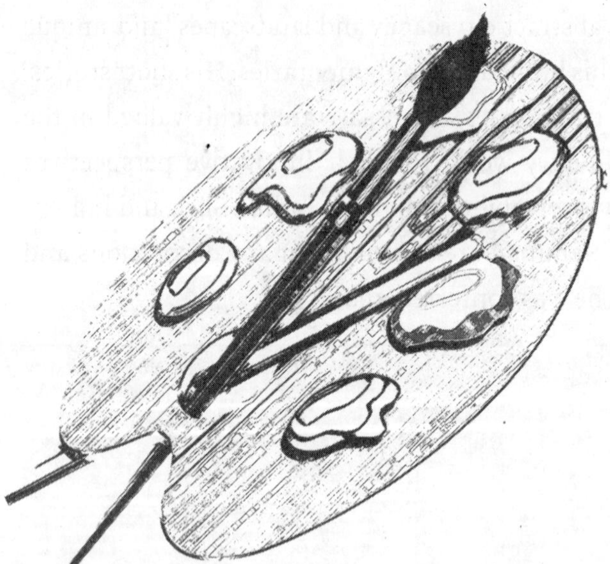

Empty Canvas

Khali Canvas

They were both sitting on the broad parapet of the terrace. No conversation passed between them, but they were used to such silences. Often their friends and acquaintances made fun of their queer quiescence.

They could catch a glimpse of the sea in front of them, behind a house. The sea sparkled bright though it was growing dark. The wind that evening was strong and puffs of clouds were hovering in the sky. Suddenly he broke into a boisterous laugh that reverberated through the calm of the evening.

'How long shall we continue to sit like this? Won't you go home today?' he wondered aloud.

'I don't feel like going home today. I want to keep sitting like this—I could pass the night this way,' she said, in a subdued voice, 'Light me a cigarette, I can't in this strong wind.'

'You are smoking too much. Yesterday I noticed an ash-tray in your studio full of half-burnt cigarettes,' he said, reaching for the cigarettes in the pocket of his trousers.

'It's not such a bad habit, though. It makes it easier to idle away the hours,' she replied.

He began pacing from one end of the terrace to the other. She smoked, sitting as before. She had been feeling exhausted in her studio. On the terrace, her weariness disappeared altogether.

'Want to listen to a record?' he asked.

'Alright, but don't play it too loud.'

He went towards his studio, which stood at the other end of the terrace, a light shining from its open window. There was a large canvas inside, fitted on the easel. He stopped for a brief moment in front of the canvas as he passed. 'How many days had it been lying in this position on the easel! I contemplate it everyday, hours on end, but dare not draw even a faint line.'

He took out a record from the almirah and put it on the gramophone. He stood a while, listening to the sounds emanating from it. Then he opened the almirah again. There was half a bottle of whisky lying in a corner. He uncorked the bottle, swallowed a large draught and came out onto the terrace. The soft sound of the music followed him.

'I was just thinking, we have passed eight years here, painting in this studio,' she said.

'Another eight will go by and we won't even know,' he answered.

'No, no. It can't be like that. If only I could, I'd stop coming here from tomorrow. You don't know how I sometimes hate this studio of mine.'

He came and sat down beside her. 'Both of us have tried to escape from this place, but failed. We come back here over and over again. Who knows, it might have been worse out there—the place to which we wanted to escape to.'

'It's fine if you can console yourself like this. But, please...let's talk about something else.'

He watched her, intently, for a while, but she had her eyes turned towards the sea.

'Did you do any work today?'

'I did do something, but it's no good. And you...did you begin on the large canvas?'

'No, it is lying there as before,' he said, 'perhaps I am haunted by my own ghost and it won't release me...'

She laughed. 'And perhaps you are my ghost from whom I can't free myself.'

He laughed too, 'May be, you are right.' Then, after a moment's pause, 'But I have done no work for months. Looks as if I must give up painting, at last. But will it be possible to take up something else now?'

'Yes, this time there has been quite a long gap. But once you start you pick up pace. Don't worry. People look forward to your exhibition,' she said, smiling at him.

'Do you think so?'

'That's a fact. What does it matter what I think. I could also be in the same position, though...'

'I have been going over all this and may be that's why I can't start my work.' He stood up and continued. 'I now know very well what my position really is, and to be honest, it's better not to work like this. But how shall I muster the courage?'

'You look at things too starkly: all this is insignificant.'

But he was grim for a long time. There were so many things on his mind and he could not concentrate on anything. They did not mean much to him and yet they engulfed him.

Suddenly he realized that the music had stopped. Perhaps it had stopped long ago, but he had not noticed it.

'Oh, I forgot to tell you something. I met Shakti yesterday. She is in town.'

'Yes, I know,' he said, softly.

'It seems her husband is quite rich. She has a house, a car, servants...everything. She talked on and on to me about all this.'

He kept quiet. He had separated permanently from Shakti only two years ago. It now seemed like history. 'She was enquiring about you too, but she seems to me to have changed a lot and rather quickly.' She could not decide about what more she should tell him in this regard.

He tried to laugh, but his attempt to do so sounded odd in the dark.

'Even today you withdraw as soon as there is any mention of Shakti, though you pretend you've forgotten everything!'

He did not protest and kept smoking in silence.

Perhaps nothing is ever erased completely. When Pramod's face looms up before her eyes—she cannot believe that it is almost three years since his death.

The wind had grown stronger. The darkness deeper. She wrapped her sari tightly around herself. It was cold now. The sound of the waves had drawn closer now.

'What's the time?'

'Must be around eight, though one hardly feels it,' he said.

'I want to rent a separate room like you have. I am tired of living with my family, year after year.'

He was used to this from her. At times, it didn't even reach his ears. Once again he realized that the record had stopped playing and he hadn't noticed it. The terror was growing invisible. The six-foot long empty canvas: his own life—flat and empty. Silly ideas badgering him all the time... He let out a long sigh.

'I have no involvement here, but...'

'When you went to London, I thought you wouldn't ever return. But then you were back within three months. How little we are able to know one another and yet we claim to know so much—I realized it only then.'

Perhaps it was a mistake to come back from there...but did he have a choice? A letter from Shakti, and he would be all anxious. He had made arrangements for an exhibition. But he could not put his heart to work. He would sit in a quiet restaurant and write long letters to Shakti. Today he laughed at his stupidity. Yet he has never once regretted it. It was a special situation and the manner in which he faced it, a special experience.

Suddenly she got to her feet, 'We have sat here far too late. Come, let's go for a stroll. The waves are so high today,' she said as she ran a comb through her hair.

He was not keen on a stroll at this hour, but it seemed unfair to refuse. He threw a parting glance at the empty canvas before he switched off the lights. Specks of dust on the canvas caught his attention for the first time... He opened the almirah, took another sip of the whisky, put off the light without any further brooding and locked the door. Yet another day was over!

There were few strollers at the beach. There were no noises, except for the sound of waves crashing against the shore. She was walking on the sands, rapt in herself, oblivious even of his presence. He made several attempts to start a conversation, then gave in to the silence. He also felt a little hungry and drowsy.

'It's good there aren't many people here today,' she broke the silence. 'How dark it is, you can't see a light for miles.'

They had had neighbouring studios for years now, they met each other several times a day. That evening she walked on and on with her eyes lowered, as if she was in a hurry to reach somewhere.

'We have come way out, it seems,' he said. 'Shall we turn back?' She strode ahead, without responding to his suggestion. He had to quicken his own pace to catch up with her. He said laughing. 'You are running away, today.'

'Will you sit for a while?' She asked suddenly.

'I think we had better go back. It's rather late. The fishermen in the village nearby are said to be bad.'

'Are you scared? Come, let's just sit for five minutes. I'm tired.' She sat down. He sat down, too, perforce, a little distance away.

'Look, there's a ship moving far away. I can see its lights,' she said.

He lighted two cigarettes and handed one to her. She smiled. 'You know my mind.'

He regarded her carefully. Ruffled hair, a simple, plain face. Everything about her face was transparent, totally devoid of secrets.

'There is one thing that often comes to my mind but it never lasts long...' he began slowly, as if weighing every word. 'I have often thought of telling you, but I couldn't muster the courage. You might even laugh at it. Sometimes I too laugh to myself. And whenever my friends talk about it, I brush it aside.' He found it very difficult to continue with the subject. Better pause for a while, he decided.

He half expected her to humorously coax him along, or to make fun of him for this mystical prologue. But she was quiet and it made him apprehensive. But now that he had broached the topic, he couldn't leave it at that.

He burst out laughing, trying to minimize the grimness. 'Of course, there are any number of absurd ideas raking one's mind, particularly when one is around 40. Maybe I'm also a victim of the same condition,' he went on.

She looked up at him as though reproachfully. Even in the dark he was able to discern a gleam in her eyes, like a flash of lightning, and it was not easy to face it.

'Several times, friends have asked...since we've known each other for so many years...has it never...between...' he faltered, but resumed at once, 'Did it never occur to us that we could together...'

He suddenly felt exhausted as though he had come to the end of a long journey. But the significance of all this had suddenly diminished. It was deathly quiet all around—at least that's what he felt. He wanted to lift her bowed head with both his hands and just have a look at it. Then she cannot hide anything, her silence itself will tell everything, he thought...but she was sitting there, like a statue, as if what he had been saying was not even remotely concerned with her.

In order to lighten the atmosphere he laughed and said, 'What funny things people think of...without a head or tail...no sense... and how can there ever be...' But he could not go on in this vein. He was unsure about the credibility of his statements.

He can't say how long after that they sat there, silent. He did not know when it was that the dusk turned into a glowing dark night. The wind grew stronger, the sound of waves turned into a wall...was it all a situation, a dream, without a trace of reality, he would wonder later.

Then a faint sound of someone weeping reached his ears. He gave a start. He peered around into the dark. There was no one there, apart from the two of them. Suddenly it seemed it was she, herself, weeping, very softly, as if it was an effort for her to weep without an apparent reason. He watched her silently, her drooping head and her hair blowing in the wind. Everything else had become vacuous. He saw the canvas loom up before his mind's eye...empty for months...but now it seemed there was no space therein. Not even for a line.

Raghuvir Sahay

Raghuvir Sahay (1928–1990) is among the most significant poets on the modern literary scene in India. Sahay belongs to a tradition of literature that defies easy classifications. A phenomenal editor who initiated a lot of youth into journalism, a social commentator and a partisan for secularism, he represents a generation that grew with the aspirations of the freedom movement. He was passionate about music and theatre. His translation of Shakespearean plays and Hungarian Poetry are especially valued.

This Way, Please!

Rasta Idhar Se Hai

It was a wretched day. It was calm and quiet here, in this room. You didn't hear the sound of a footstep on the floor richly laid with carpets. The walls smooth, tranquil, like marble. The temperature constant, just right from the health point of view, and, to top it all, no dust. You could stretch your limbs with your sleeves on the table. Quite unlike in the rooms below, where they spread out their ledgers and registers even as the leftovers of their tiffin were wiped off the tables.

All the same, it was a wretched day.

In all, 40 people had walked in and out of the room, one after the other. Forty! Ali Baba, open up Sim-Sim! There was a door for entry just as there was one for exit. However, there was a third door too, which if opened, led nowhere. Even if one opened it and crossed its threshold, he was bound to return after having answered a short or long call of nature. However, there was nothing written on it which would indicate where it led to. As soon as the person sitting in front of us got up in order to leave the room, he tried to open this third door. And each time this happened, we, the five men sitting in the room, called out in unison, our fingers pointing in the direction of the right door: 'This way, Please!'

Both the doors looked exactly alike. We would never have opened that door 40 times, even if all five of us had had to sit all day through, our genuine need to ease ourselves notwithstanding. But on that particular day it was opened 40 times and yet no one took a step beyond. It was barely opened when all five of us would cry out the words quoted above. A glimpse of the shining commode, and instantly the door would be slammed with a click. The person who ventured to open the door would turn around and make for the right door, his head bowed low.

There was something unusual about it. No sooner did we finish with our interlocution, the man who had been let in would grow so anxious to dart out of the room that he would invariably spot that very door, behind which lurked a commode. After the scene had been repeated several times over, all five of us began to laugh. One of us wondered aloud, 'Has the company set it up as a test for them?' Probably he thought it was a nice contraption to test out one's personality traits. Did he, the man who came seeking employment, get so nervous that he forgot which door he had entered through? Said another, 'Ha ha ha ha!' A third one opined, 'No, originally it wasn't meant for this. You do have a point in what you say, however. Let us set aside five marks for this, too.' The fourth man said, 'But who shall be given the marks? One who goes out through the right door?' Upon this I said, 'No, not him. Instead, let us award five marks to him who opens the door to the toilet inadvertently, and upon hearing us exclaim, 'No, this way, please,' turns around and retorts, 'I know, sir. I was only going to ease myself.'

This idea, however, did not find favour with anyone. The water closet was supposed to be used for pissing by the general manager only. And if there was a conference of the general manager, the assistant general manager and the chief deputy assistant general manager, and during the conference, if the chief deputy assistant general manager were to be assailed by an urge to pee, it was not quite clear if he could use the toilet which was reserved for the GM. The assistant general manager, though, would possibly be justified in going in, with the permission of the GM. On the other hand, the chief deputy assistant general manager would have to go out, although it is true that the distance to be covered in his sojourn to his own room, attached with a toilet, would not be more than the length of his own designation.

Nobody had liked my idea and so I was a little dejected. If someone had supported me, I could have suggested a few more innovations. For example, full marks would be given to one who would actually go into the toilet room and piss, but not to those who merely said so.

Of course, it would have been quite in order for my colleagues to improvise further. For example, the first amongst us could have suggested that we award one mark if the candidate made no noise while making water; another mark could be given if he buttoned up his trousers inside the toilet, rather than while emerging from it; and all of us could have agreed to nullify all marks if a candidate in pajamas rolled it up in the process.

Instead, they began to quibble over the fact that we had not until then included this in the tests, and that it would be unjust and discriminatory at this stage. So far, the candidates had been questioned to test their fluency in English. And we, the five arbiters, had been judicious at least in this respect. We knew that speaking English could not be put at par with one's deftness at opening a toilet door.

We were the topmost officers in that building. We all had our separate office rooms. We were served an exclusive lunch every afternoon which was far superior to the food served in the office canteen. Curiously enough, from this it had been concluded that we all needed exclusive rooms for pissing and shitting as well, though evidently, in spite of our better food, we couldn't have performed any better in there than those who ate the coarse canteen meals. It occurred to me that if there was an agitation for equality in this building, it would not be successful even if the demand for common food for all had been met. Brooding over the reasons for the failure of all such movements, I concluded that they failed mainly because they never put up a demand for common toilets for all.

We had gathered here to select salesmen for our fountain pen manufacturing company. Now, look at this boy sitting before us. He is being asked why he wants to take up this work. All other routine questions have been asked. For example, what are your hobbies? To every question asked, the candidates squeeze out the best in their personality, as though everything depended on the appropriate answer to that single question. To tell the truth, this was not at all the case. But none of them had the foggiest idea about the actual criterion applied for the selection of the candidate. Those who had secured less than 50 marks in the written test were dismissed after just one question: 'Why do you want to take up this work?' If someone tried to invent a grandiose answer, his fate was sealed. For example, 'I want to disseminate knowledge by selling pens.' On the other hand, if one said, 'Because I am looking for a suitable job,' he would be countered with, 'Why this particular job?' A simple answer to this question was rare to come by. They always tried to spell out a grand cause. And we knew that would sound the knell for their hope. We also knew that no one would have the courage to plainly admit that he wanted a job because of the vacancy (of the post as well as his own). This was the precise truth and nobody could have had a reason better than that for appearing in an interview for a job.

Now this boy said that he actually wanted to go into law, but he had second thoughts—he might not be able to get along, after all. With these words he landed himself into a trap. Promptly the question was flung at him: How can you canvass for pens if you cannot plead for clients? This made him nervous and tremulously he replied, 'I'll manage it somehow.' For a fleeting second I tried to visualize this boy hawking in a crowd: 'Buy the fountain pen of the Bharat Company—it always writes the truth.'

Another boy. He belonged to a family of traditional shopkeepers. Making himself comfortable in the chair, his looks seemed to proclaim: just give me a chance to be your salesman, and one of these days I will buy off the company itself. The GM was most pleased with that boy in spite of a great personal risk looming before his eyes. He enquired about the health, etc. of his father and even offered him tea. The next thing, I suspected, would be to invite him to use his private toilet. However, he didn't.

Several other candidates poured in one after the other. All of them had studied literature, science, politics, economics, history or law—one or the other of these subjects—in various universities. It was in fact an essential qualification for the job. Some of them had come clad in perhaps their best clothes. But note their shoes, gentlemen, note the shoes, not clothes—I wanted to tell my co-panelists. You can judge one's true character by his shoes alone. For example, the shoes of one candidate clearly betrayed his poor family background although there was polish on them. The shoes of another man left you in no doubt that he owned several more pairs, while his clothes were quite ordinary. You see, that is the way an aristocrat usually carries himself about. Ordinary clothes... but his shoes, you know!

There were one or two candidates who said that they wanted a job so that they could lighten the burden on the shoulders of their old man. Three boys wanted employment because they found it humiliating to live as dependents of their brothers. But such reasons as these would simply not do with them, for no wonders could be expected of such young men in the marketing of pens.

There was one among them who just did not give any reason for wanting the job. He merely got up from his chair and began to pray: 'Sir, please give me a job. It will be highly kind of you, sir.'

The most important thing that our general manager told us later was, that no candidate was able to tell the height of the TV tower in West Germany. The GM had recently returned from a visit and he was still under the spell of the tower with a restaurant on the top.

We were measuring up the candidates with the yardsticks of their hobbies, shoes, clothes, fluency in English and so on, and showing them the door with an orchestrated: 'This way, please!' The day was drawing to a close. It was time to make a list of successful candidates. The secretary to the GM brought in a chart showing the marks obtained by them.

After appropriate tabulation, we found that none of them was suitable for appointment. It had already been decided that only those who secured more than 70 marks would be considered for selection, but they were all far below the target and so we decided to re-advertise the posts.

Learning from this experience, we now stipulated yet another condition in the advertisement—those who were not already employed need not apply. It proved to be useful in several ways. The main advantage was that in the second round, we did not have to exclaim 'This way, please!' Candidates walked in and immediately made it obvious in a refined manner that they knew that the adjacent room was nothing but a toilet. The proceedings of course now became rather monotonous on this account. However, we finally picked up a man who, in the course of the interview, had abruptly interjected with: 'Excuse me, sir. I'll just be a minute.'

A Chant

Kirtan

After having lived twelve years in this city, he realized that he had got himself acquainted with such a large number of people that now it was beyond him to strike the kind of natural relationship which should be possible between two persons as they run into each other. But then he wondered if he himself was aware of what he had lost? There is hardly anybody around who would appreciate the kind of relationship he would have cherished to have for a short while, lasting just as long as the glow would last between him and his chance companion. These days, people either raise their hand in a perfunctory greeting as if striving to flick off themselves an oncoming touch, or they just want to trap you in something utterly selfish; like two persons groping for their own lubricants in one another—ultimately they would both get fattened and exhausted and fall apart like the contented leeches.

Somehow it happened again, and it was all too usual with him, that he had been walking for long trying to sort this puzzle out.

Tiredness invariably renders me lonely, and just think how essential it is, this loneliness, this tiresomeness, in a city like this—long distances, desolate people, and dull-witted officials... It is just as well that I am not riding a fast vehicle and I am making up the time with my own labour, he thought.

His body was clammy with sweat. How nice to let your body sweat profusely! You feel with your body like a common animal and all your inner movements become a part of the carnal process itself. The odour of his sweat had not yet reached his nostrils—he was not that exhausted as yet—but he was able to recognize the odour inwardly. And presently his own face with its sharp features sprang up before his mind's eye.

The place he was going to was the house of an eccentric doctor. He was the only person in the entire city whom he had known neither more nor less. Just enough, as two adults with their own separate worlds ought to know one another. He would set out from his home repeating to himself all sorts of symptoms and he would describe each of them so vividly that it seemed as if he were unraveling a deep mystery about the conduct of the human body. Although the doctor had gone senile and at times would conclude after listening to a long narration of the difficulty in one's left nostril that it was the right nostril that needed treatment, he never lost his cool in trying to convince the doctor. He would repeat his tale again as if to avert the terrible crime that might befall humanity if a prescription of medicine were made on the basis of wrong symptoms. And this time his speech would shed all its redundant words without any hint of pettiness, of pitying the doctor. The doctor was handsome and old, whose little dishonesties in a long life could be forgiven. His face was ever ready with a fresh curiosity.

As he approached the doctor's house his tiredness had grown to such a degree that he almost parted with his child and the condition in which he had left him at home began to appear as an understandable phenomenon. The child was in fact very ill and he was a fragile child. Among the fragile ones too he belonged to the category of those who dissipate from within when ill, and yet appear quite clear-headed and sharp at the end. I can't tell exactly what torment Montoo must be undergoing at this moment. I know now even less than I had known a while ago. Suddenly the child turned into a fully developed man, a being, capable to shoulder his own responsibility. He stepped into the doctor's house as if reading out something in bold type.

It was filled with an aroma there. No need to inhale deep; it was all over there, motionless. He then sensed a slight stir nearby. A few voices. The voices had a rhythm. Perhaps they were chanting a hymn. The verandah was covered with a white sheet. Denuding his feet of his slippers, he sat down on the sheet. On one side of him a woman of wheatish complexion was sitting with her hair in the armpits cropped short and with her wrists full of red bangles. There were several persons beyond as well as before her. And he viewed them each to the extent they fell in the range of his vision and when he had surveyed the whole scene he found that the picture was perfect.

Except for one man in a blue-striped shirt who seemed 'wrong' to him. However, that man soon got up and walked away into the house and so no harm was done.

A peculiar resonance was falling upon his ears as if the chant had just come to an end or maybe it was about to begin. One of the two things. Seating himself on his knees he tried to imagine his own face. The same face of his choice materialized. Then he glanced in turn at the visible portions of each face and when he had finished, there came a thump on the *mridangam.*

The thumps on the *mridangam* continued. It seemed as if each of the thump had a set purpose. Something, maybe it was the sound of *mridangam,* began revealing itself as if deliberately. The aroma belongs to *loban* (incense), he concluded.

Should he so wish, just by rising a bit, he could look over the place from where the *swara* (musical note) was coming and find out what was there. But it was of no use, he thought. This is the crowd in which I am and the jingle is also in the same crowd and it has just unraveled its own features. In a wink it was clear that he was also in it. Or, he should not have been there.

There was some stir in the front portion of the gathering. A very tall man rose and gathered his pleated dhoti and went inside, treading his way cautiously through the crowd. He had six toes on one of his feet.

No, the music did not keep pace with him. There was no narrative in the music which would keep pace with that movement, instead it was turning out in jingles, and more jingles.

He heard some words, too. 'Rama', 'Krishna'. He failed to grasp anything from the name of 'Rama'. 'Krishna' was a bit more comprehensible. The way it was undulating with stress on the compound letter. He was able to grasp just that.

The words picked up speed again, then merged into each other, and then broke off abruptly. Only the rhythm, like a soul freed from the body continued to reverberate, balance, wind, spiral up higher and higher. All alone, it grew more and more intense. Once again the words returned. 'Krishna' was still more distinct this time. It seemed to him that among all those words he was able to hear only that, or maybe it was the beats of the *mridangam,* not a linguistic word. Now there was no smell; only the breeze blew in with a dash of it. This time he succeeded in spotting out the man who had lit the incense. He was enjoying his work. I hate this man, he decided at once.

The jingle now sounded as if a spinning top had gone asleep. The fair coloured woman sitting next to him stretched out her arms, putting her elbows on her knees, and she was holding one of her wrists with her other hand. It was at the focal point of her sitting figure that she had grasped her wrist, and that's just where there originated a tension in her wiry thighs. Her fingers looked blunted and there was a largish brown spot on one of her cheeks, but she was sitting so peacefully with her entire lovely body that there was no need to look up for her face. She had soft fine hair on her white back and it seemed as if she were feeling everything with them. The armpit with cropped hair where the skin had grown a little darker was open like a window to glance into her.

A man from the crowd got on to his feet and began dancing. He did not want to communicate anything through his body. He had released it, just because he found it difficult to hold. The *mridangam* beats passed by him in circles. The woman sitting near the fragrance-man let out a shriek. Nobody paid any heed.

This was a fat black woman and she had a long-sleeved chequered *salooka* (blouse) on her. Then it seemed as though, she too had got up to dance, but it was not so. The man, who was bent upon frittering away the upsurge in his body, gave out heavy and clumsy jerks to his limbs above the waist. *Loban*. Its smell reminds you of a fresh corpse with several men on the vigil, he thought.

Suddenly he noticed the doctor emerge. He was not a party to the jingle called *kirtan*. The doctor called out to him as if from across a wide river under an overcast sky. He did not go to the doctor who was surrounded by a motley crowd.

I hate him too, he said, as he saw a skinny youth. This is a thief. I hate every one of them. I hated them all, not after I came here, but always. I hated some without any reason, but some others not without one. I am, however, not obliged to tell if there is a reason. I don't like them, I don't like them, I don't like... However the *chogun chhand*—the galloping jingle of the chant—was slowing down. I'll go against it, he resolved for a moment. Let me see what happens when one accepts defeat. No, slowing down of the rhythm is not my necessity. Not even theirs taken together. It's only his who is singing in the main *swara*, and I hate him, too.

His struggle was getting intense again. I hate everyone that I can hate. But not this flock! Suddenly he knew they had nothing to do with him. But there is something due to which neither I can shake them off, nor they me. Certainly it is not devotion, he proclaimed in a flash. Jingle, maybe, but most probably not; crowd, yes, but not merely that.

Perhaps my body. Also the woman's body. Damp with sweat, tired, sunken, strained body—mine and her and his, their bodies, too, perhaps! Each of the free bodies. Churned up. Each throbbing with whatever stuff it contained. Closed, protected, purely a carnal being. Expelling its own filth and spattering it all over the hairy skin.

Anything might happen at this moment, he said. And just by itself. Any happening might take place this moment just for the sake of it. My child might die. Or I might die. Dying is the only happening the body could perform most perfectly at this moment, its finest creation in its own unique way.

The doctor came in sight again. This time he nodded, as if in agreement.

People rose to their feet, making movements in proportion to their weight; their clothes below the waist showed distinct creases, each with a different calligraphy. One of them yawned and the *mridangam* fell silent. He now noticed that a shining pair of brass *manjiras* (cymbals) was also lying there, and not only that, it had all along accompanied the *mridangam*.

He stood up. He put on his slippers before setting his feet on the bare floor and stood still for an instant with his weight on his one leg. It had no significance. It was a habit with him. On occasions, though, it seemed as if it enabled him to disengage himself.

By the time he arrived home it had all become a thing of the past. The door was opened by his wife. She looked plumper in her straight flank of sari, her head covered. He was not able to see her face. The woman pointed to the room. His child lay straight in perfect peace. Somebody had covered him with white cloth from head to foot, but curiously his heels were showing.

The Victor

Vijeta

The room where she had delivered the baby was filled with the mixed odour of burning *ajwain* and bitter oil, and she was lying there wrapped in clean old clothes. He paused as he reached the door. He would find her there. Changed, but in what state after what has happened to her? And he, too, would be there, whom he has so often felt in Kamini's body, between her and himself, and independent of them both. Would he be aware of what I have done to him? I am eager to see him, knowing well that I had not wanted him and yet I hope, thought Ashok, he has forgiven me, for I have only love for him, if love is the word to express even a modicum of what I have in my heart.

They were both averse to having children at present. They might have reasoned differently, to be sure, but it hardly mattered, for both of them had very definite views about the uses of their body. He too did not want this to happen, but that which had come to pass was ultimately due to him only and so his consort was pregnant. It is I who has done this and she is my woman and she does not want this and I, the stronger of the two, am the cause of this. It will be all right, he said with a laugh. He had produced a terrible-looking bottle, it was something dark and brownish, with a bitter reek, he had smelt it and said, his eyes half-closed, you'd love this and it would be a good riddance.

For two days, Kamini had been convulsing with a burning sensation all over her body, as if a furnace deep within her had been lit. Nevertheless she waited patiently. She would open her eyes to look about herself, but all she could see was drowned in a dark red. Has it begun? She would wonder when again it would all go dead within her and she would doze off. After two days, she got up stealthily, didn't utter a word and plunged into work, and so a few more days passed.

Didn't it work? Asked Ashok, I had been told that it would, but may be you require something stronger. And he smiled as if tickling the woman.

I'll set everything right, don't be scared.

What can you do? she said.

Why, if I could do one thing. I could also do another.

What a foul mouth he had, thought Kamini, and she had a feeling of nausea.

Why are you nervous? You will feel some pain, that's all.

This time it was a few innocuous white pills and again Kamini had to turn and toss in blazing fever continually for four days. She would open her mouth like a bird and gasp and she wanted only to fly away. And for a time she felt she had arrived into a void, fell down several times from up there, and regained consciousness; yet she had to keep lying down, for the thing was running in all directions like molten metal inside her and refused to get out.

God has saved me, she said.

Silly talk, said Ashok, your body could withstand this pain, because it was strong.

Was she indeed alone in bearing the pain? Surely it couldn't have been. 'I won't die,' she said, 'for now I don't want to die.'

You won't die, you have just to visit the doctor once.

No, no, she said, I won't go.

Just once you will feel a little pain, then it'll be all right.

No, no said Kamini. For myself I could have said, yes, let there be pain, but can I decide for someone else? Now I won't allow you to do anything, she said.

Silly, so far it hasn't even acquired life.

But it has, said Kamini; it was a thing you wanted to destroy but it was not destroyed, proving that it existed. I know that it exists and you have attacked it twice and it has escaped these attacks. The resistance it must have put up!—marvelled Kamini, and looked with pity at her husband.

I know you are stronger than it, but you have been defeated. Now you let it be, she said, for it has begun to be, and added, in her own mind, it shall be and it shall forgive you.

Ashok glanced inside as he took a step forward. There was only a glow of the oil lamp in front of him, and a peculiar cleanliness, the two linked to each other, and alive.

Where are they? He asked himself. Until as recently as yesterday she had been carrying him along with herself up to that moment which she alone could experience. For hours on end they had exchanged anecdotes of their childhood, and she would sit there, heavy and tired, pure and calm; you must stay by me, she had said. Of course, Ashok had said at last without knowing why, but then he didn't have any other place to go, he thought, and so he was there, close at hand, passing, within himself, through the experience through which his wife had to pass with her entire body.

He took two steps forward. He was there—nay, both of them were there. He sat down on an edge, twisting his huge body at several points. Kamini was on the bed with her back to him. There she is, my woman, so pretty and fresh. If only this distance between us would stay on forever!

Suddenly he remembered his child. Let me see, he said.

Kamini looked up. At first she blushed and turned her face toward the child as if hiding herself, then set her eyes mockingly on his father.

Why, what is so special in me? asked Ashok.

Nothing, I am just watching what a man looks like, said Kamini to herself, and uncovered the face of the child.

Ashok's heart thumped fiercely. How would he look like? Cheerful? Or would be recalling what I have done to him? Forgiven me? Forgive me, he said, and his face beamed.

With clenched red fists and his woman's breast in his mouth, the child was effortlessly enjoying his prerogative. There wasn't a single scar on him, neither a scratch, nor a blot, nothing. He is the victor, said Ashok, and his face flushed with suppressed laughter.

The boy didn't so much as glance at his father, nor did he know who he was or what he wanted. He didn't have to, indeed. With his eyes closed he was busy with his work, lying there like a pumpkin. He had won a battle and he was there, intact and complete, just the way he had been made in spite of the others, and that was all that concerned him at the moment.

Nirmal Verma

Nirmal Verma (1929–2005) pioneered the Nayi Kahani literary movement in Hindi literature in the late 1950s with his iconic story *Parinde*. He developed a characteristic style which used rich, poetic description as a mirror of the inner life. Following his work at the Oriental Institute in Prague in the 1960s, he undertook direct translations of contemporary Czech writers such as Milan Kundera, Bohumil Hrabal and Václav Havel into Hindi, much before their work became internationally popular. His honours include India's highest literary award, the Jnanpith (2000); India's third-highest civilian award, the Padma Bhushan (2003); and the Sahitya Akademi Fellowship (1985), apart from several national and international Fellowships.

The World Elsewhere

Doosari Duniya

Long ago I knew a girl who played all day in the park. There were many trees in the park but I could name only a few. I would spend the whole day in the library and, in the evening, when I came out I would find her sitting among those trees. We did not speak to one another for many days. I frequently place-changed those days for cheaper accommodation and had settled down in that corner of London only for a short time.

London seemed wretched and I felt low most of the time.

The girl in the park looked no better. She was always in a threadbare sweater. An auburn cap covered her head, but her hair tripped out rebelliously from both sides. Her ears and the tip of her nose seemed a permanent red as those were the last days of October—days just short of winter—and, sometimes these early days were more cruel than the actual winter.

I went to the library only to thaw out my frozen bones. At night, before retiring, I'd wrap myself in all my sweaters and socks and for additional comfort, I'd pile my coats and overcoat on top of the quilt—but still the cold would not go. Not that there was no heater in the room, but it took a shilling to light it. The first night I slept in that room, I fed the bloody thing with my shillings throughout the night—I had no money even for my breakfast on the morning after. Then I left the heater alone. I shivered through the nights, but I had the consolation that the heater too lay there—cold and starving. And so the cold-war continued between us night after night.

With the first hint of the morning, I'd hurry over to the library. I've lost count of the many others who, like me, were regulars there. They stood in a queue long before the door of the library opened. They were mostly old people who received a meagre pension. They'd open a book or two and settle down at the table. After a while I'd hear them snoring softly. No one disturbed them. Occasionally, an employee of the library would go round, close the open books and gently pat those whose snores disturbed the sleep or study of others.

On one such slumbering noon I saw that girl from one of the windows of the library. She had put her satchel on a bench and hid herself behind the trees. It was a cloudy afternoon and she was all alone. The other benches were empty. And that day, for the first time, I became intensely curious to know of the games children play when they are all alone.

She would come to the park at noon, put her satchel on the bench and run away behind the trees. Now and then I would raise my head from the book and watch her. The hospital clock would chime at five and the girl, wherever she was, would rush and return to her bench. She would hold the satchel in her lap and wait with deceptive calm till she discovered a woman walk towards her from the other direction. I could never see the face of the woman. She was always in the white uniform of a nurse. But before she could wend her way to the bench, the girl would run and meet her halfway. They would turn towards the gate and my eyes would follow them until they had both disappeared from my sight. All this I watched, like a Hitchcock hero, out of the window, where this pantomime was repeated every day. This scenario would have continued, perhaps all through the winter, had the weather not taken a turn.

One night I suddenly felt choked under the weight of my quilt and coats. I was perspiring as if I had recovered after a long bout of fever. I opened the window and peered out. There was no mist or fog; the London sky lay open like a blue velvet-box filled with stars. I felt as though it were a summer-night and I was lying on the terrace of my own home.

The next day was gloriously warm. I could not sit in the library for long. I got out at noon and walked down to the restaurant where I ate every day. It was a cheap Jewish restaurant where one could get kosher meat, two slices of bread and a small glass of beer for just a shilling and a half. The Jewish proprietress who came from Lithuania before the war, sat on a high stool. The cash-box lay on the counter; a Siamese cat crouched under it staring at the customers. She blinked at me with her little green eyes as I ate. Perhaps, she had begun to recognize me. Even a cat, I reflected, is a great help in times of destitution and loneliness. Someday, my thoughts completed their circuit; I, too, would set up an Indian restaurant, and keep three cats as pets.

Coming out of the restaurant, I lost the desire to go back to the library. I had received letters and newspapers from home after a long time. I wanted to read them in the park's sunlight. I was a little surprised to see flowers in the park. They were tiny flowers, their heads bravely erect in the grass. Perhaps, it was these flowers that Jesus had called 'lilies of the field'—flowers that do not despair of the morrow.

They reminded you of a long gone summer.

I walked on the flowers scattered in the grass.

It was very pleasant. Nightmares of the future were forgotten. I felt light. I slipped my shoes off and began to walk barefoot in the park. I was almost near the bench when I heard a shriek behind me. Somebody was rushing towards me. I turned—it was the same girl. She emerged from the cluster of trees and blocked my way.

'You are caught!' She was all excitement. 'You cannot escape now.'

I didn't understand. I stood still where I was.

'You've been caught,' she repeated, 'you are standing on my land.'

I looked around—there was the grass, the flowers, empty benches on one side, three evergreen trees and an oak-tree with a heavy trunk in the centre. There was no trace of her land anywhere.

'Sorry,' I said and turned to leave.

'No, no...you can't go,' the little girl stood barring my way. Her eyes were shining. 'They won't let you go.'

'Who won't let me go?' I asked.

She pointed to the trees, which now took on the appearance of tall and sturdy guards. Unwittingly I had fallen into their invisible trap.

We stood facing one another for some moments. Her gaze was fixed on me—excited and alert. When she saw that I had no intention of fleeing, she relaxed.

'Do you want to be released?' she said.

'How?' I looked at her.

'You'll have to give them food. They have been hungry for many days,' she pointed to the trees. Their woolly heads shook against the breeze.

'I don't have food with me,' I said.

'You could bring some if you want to,' she advised. 'They eat only flowers and leaves.'

It was not difficult. Those were the days of October when, besides flowers, there were plenty of leaves scattered all over the park. Just as I stooped she sprang forward to intercept my hand.

'No, no...not from here. This is my land. You'll have to go over there,' she gestured towards the park fencing, where wizened leaves lay in a heap. I started in that direction when she called.

'Please, wait...I'll come with you, but should you try to escape...you will die at once.' She stopped, looked at me, 'Do you want to die?'

Hastily I shook my head. It was such a warm and bright day that I had no wish to do any such thing.

We went up to the fence. I took out my handkerchief to collect the flowers and the leaves. It was the least I could do to buy my freedom.

She was quiet as we walked back. I glanced at her from the corner of my eye. She seemed to be a sickly child. Grim, as children are who play alone. Her lips twitched when she was silent—the lower lip protruded slightly, above which her pug nose appeared pathetically helpless. Her hair too short, and too black, parted like the rings of washed cotton, and there was this uncontrollable urge to touch them.

'Now you may feed them.' She had stopped near the trees.

'Would they release me?' I wanted some guarantee, some kind of assurance.

This time she smiled and, for the first time, I noticed her teeth—pure white and shining, the kind black girls have.

I took the leaves from my handkerchief, divided them into four parts and distributed them equally at the foot of the trees.

I was free—and somewhat empty, too.

I took out the letters and newspapers from my pocket and sat down on the bench where her satchel lay—a black leather satchel crammed with books and a half nibbled apple straining out of its upper pocket.

She had vanished. Cautiously I looked around and caught the briefest glimpse of her frock behind the shrubs. She was crouching like a rabbit, ready to pounce upon another straggler like me. But no one passed that way for long. The leaves, deposited under the trees, swirled like an eddy as the wind blew—and she ran after them, forgetting her ambush.

She came to the bench after sometime, regarded me for a moment and took the apple out of her bag. I heard her munch the apple as I read my papers.

Suddenly she noticed my letters lying on the bench. Her jaws stopped moving.

'These are yours?'

'Yes.' I looked at her.

'And this?'

She pointed to a stamp on the envelope, inscribed with a picture of an elephant, its trunk raised high in salute. The space between its tusks suggested laughter.

'Have you ever been to the zoo?' I asked.

'Once with papa. He gave me a penny and the elephant picked it up from my palm with his trunk.'

'Weren't you scared?'

'No, why?' she looked at me, nibbling her apple.

'Doesn't papa come here with you?'

'He had come once. And was caught thrice.'

She chuckled—oblivious of my presence—as one would in solitude where a single memory peels off the past in layers.

We were both startled when the hospital clock chimed the hour. The girl picked up her satchel from the bench and walked alongside the trees which stood in silence. She went to each tree, touched it and muttered something which only the trees could hear. Finally she came to me and shook my hand, as though I were also a tree in that family of trees.

She glanced back. I looked to see who it was and saw the woman. The familiar white uniform of a nurse gleamed in the sun. As always, the girl ran to accost her midway. I took in the details—this was the woman I had watched from the library window. Short of stature, a bag slung over her shoulder and curly black hair like the girl's. They were some distance from me but their voices floated back as a muffled suggestion of two sounds and not as words articulated separately. They sat down on the grass. The girl had forgotten me.

I wore my shoes and put the letters and papers in my pocket. There is yet time I thought. I could still spend an hour or two in my solitary corner at the library away from the magic of the park.

I ambled over to the centre of the park. The stems of the trees were aglow and the entire park melted in gold. In the centre, a river of leaves rippled in the breeze.

'Who, who is there?' Someone was calling me. I walked on. I did not stop. Sometimes a person calls out to seduce himself to step inside while there is only a void within. But this call was different—unlike that of other days. It did not cease. It forced me to stop. There was no doubt this time. Someone was really shouting, 'Stop, stop...', I turned around—the girl was waving her hands in the air.

Indeed I was caught again! Like a fool I had trespassed on her land, surrounded by the four trees, for the second time. The mother and daughter were both laughing this time.

It was a false summer. Everyone knew it wouldn't last long. The library was deserted. My neighbours, the cold pensioners, sat outside in the sun. The sky was so blue that even the London smog could not dirty it. The park underneath lay like a green island.

Greta (that was her name) would be there all day. Even when she was out of sight, her satchel on the bench hinted of her presence somewhere, perhaps, crouching in some corner. I walked warily, wary of the trees, the shrubs, the flowers on the grass. Everyday she would leave some invisible dangerous trap, and when, for all my caution, I put my foot into it, she would emerge from nowhere screaming madly. I was caught, released, caught again...

It wasn't a game. It was a world in itself. I had nothing to do with that world—though I was permitted entry sometimes, like an extra in a drama. I had to be ready all the time, for she could summon me any moment. One afternoon we were both sitting on the bench. Abruptly she stood up.

'Hello, Mrs Thomas...' she said with a smile, 'I haven't seen you for a long time... Meet him, this is my Indian friend.'

I watched her dumbfounded. There was nobody there.

'What's the matter with you? Shake her hand,' she scolded.

I stood up and shook hands with the empty air. Greta sidled closer to me to make room for Mrs Thomas.

'Were you going shopping?' she said, glancing at the empty spot. 'I guessed from your bag. No, excuse me, I can't come with you. I've got a lot of work. Look at them (she signaled towards the trees), they are hungry since morning, I haven't yet cooked for them. Will you take tea? Coffee? Oh, you've had some at home. I beg your pardon—why do I not come to your house? Where is the time these days! Hospital in the mornings, afternoons with the kids, you know how it is. I'll come on Sunday. What, are you already leaving?'

She stood up and shook her hand again. Perhaps Mrs Thomas was in a hurry, she did not notice me as she took leave. In turn, I remained seated.

For some time we sat in silence. Then suddenly she started.

'Do you hear something?' she shook my elbow.

'No, nothing,' I said.

'The telephone—how long has it been ringing! Please see who it is.'

I rose and went behind the bench, picked up a twig and said aloud, 'Hello!'

'Who is calling?' she asked anxiously.

'Mrs Thomas,' I said.

'Oh, Mrs Thomas again!' She yawned wearily, dragged herself to me with slow steps, snatched the twig from my hand and said, 'Hello, Mrs Thomas—you're back from the market? What did you buy? Meatballs and fish-fingers and potato-chips?' Her eyes widened with interest. Perhaps she was picking the delicacies of her own choice.

Then she fell silent, as if Mrs Thomas had made an unexpected offer. 'All right, Mrs Thomas, I'm coming right away. No, I won't take long. I am on my way to the bus-station. See you soon, Mrs Thomas.'

She beamed at me. 'Mrs Thomas has invited me to dinner—what will you do?'

'I'll sleep.'

'First give them something to eat, lest they cry.' She pointed to the trees which stood motionless in the still air.

She started getting ready. She combed her disheveled hair, powdered her face in a splendid mime and held up her palm to see her mirrored reflection. Caught between the sunlight and the shade of the trees, she really looked beautiful.

She waved a goodbye as she went. I watched her until she disappeared among the trees beyond the hedges of the park.

This became a daily routine. She'd go to visit Mrs Thomas and I'd lie on the bench. I didn't feel lonesome. I was always surrounded by the invisible voices of the park. I'd pillow my head on the library-books and lie down. I'd watch the clouds over London—gliding aimlessly and casting dark shadows in the park each time a stray white patch drifted over the sun.

One such day when I was lying on the bench, I heard a strange rustle beside me. I felt as though I were watching Mrs Thomas in a dream; she was close—very close—to me and calling me.

I woke up with a start.

In front of me stood Greta's mother, holding her hand and staring at me awkwardly.

'Excuse me,' she said, embarrassed, 'I hope I didn't disturb your sleep.'

I stood up, brushing my clothes.

'You're early today,' I said. The sight of her white uniform, black belt and hair, held together by a scarf, dazzled me. It seemed she had arrived straight from the hospital.

'Yes, I'm early,' she smiled. 'There isn't much work on Saturday and I come here in the afternoon.'

She spoke with a broad West Indian drawl in which the last syllable of each word took off like a balloon.

'I came to ask if you'd like to come home with us for tea today. We live nearby.'

There was no hesitation or pretence in her tone, as though she had known me for ages.

I agreed. I had not been to anybody's home for a long time. I had been shuttling between my bed-sitter, the library and the park. I'd almost forgotten that there was a world beyond—where Greta lived and ate and slept.

She walked ahead of us. Now and then she looked back to make sure we were not lagging too far behind. Greta, perhaps, felt a little odd that I was on my way to her house. I felt odd too—not because I was going to her house, but because I was walking along with her mother. She looked quite young, possibly on account of her height. She looked so petite walking beside me that I had the illusion of walking with another Greta.

She was quiet on the way. Only when we reached their house, did she abruptly stop.

'You also live somewhere here?'

'In Bride street,' I said, 'just opposite the tube station.'

'Perhaps you've moved in recently,' she said, smiling, 'there are very few Indians in this area.'

She started climbing down. Her home was in the basement and we had to descend the staircase to get there. Greta was already there, holding the door open for us. It was dark inside the room even during daytime. Three or four chairs swam into view when the light was switched on. There was a table in the middle—longer than was necessary and bare—as if used for playing ping-pong. Close to the wall lay a sofa, a quilt neatly folded at its headrest. It looked like an all-purpose room, meant for eating, sleeping and, on occasions, entertaining the guests.

'Please sit down. I'll just get the tea.'

She raised the curtain and went in. Greta and I remained alone in the room. We had started recognizing each other in the autumnal light of the park. But inside the room we had become strangers.

She had suddenly turned into a very young child whose magic and terror had both withered away.

'Do you sleep here?' I looked at the sofa.

'No, not here,' she shook her head, 'my room is inside—would you like to see it?'

There was a smallish room opposite the kitchen which must have functioned as a store in the past. It was behind a blue chick on which hung a bluish placard saying 'Keep Britain tidy, but leave my room alone!' She raised the chick and stole inside.

'Please come quietly, he's asleep'.

'Who?'

'Hush!' she put her hand on her mouth.

I thought there was someone inside. But the room was empty. The walls of the room were green, pasted with pictures of animals. In the corner was her cot which looked like a crib. A teddy bear was lying on the pillow, wrapped in rags, like a cameo.

'He's asleep,' she whispered.

'And you?' I asked, 'don't you sleep here?'

'I do. When Papa was here, he used to sleep on another bed. Ma has now had that bed put away.'

'Where does he live?' This time my voice was also soft, not for any fear of the bear, but because of a fear I had been rearing in myself for many days.

'In his home—where else?'

She looked at me with some amazement. She felt that I had not been satisfied completely. She went up to her table where her schoolbooks were kept. She opened a drawer and produced a bunch of letters. Tied with a red ribbon, it looked like a Christmas gift. She brought the bunch to me and gestured to the stamp on the top envelope.

'He lives here,' she said simply. She was mimicking me. I recalled—long ago in the park, I had shown her a letter from my country.

Her mother was calling us from the sitting room. She went out as soon as she heard the voice.

I did not move for some time. The bear was sleeping on the cot. The eyes of the animals on the wall stared back at me. There was a small basin by her bed where she kept her toothbrush, soap and comb.

Just like my own bed-sitter, I remembered. Yet altogether different. I could leave my room and go anywhere, but hers looked almost eternal in its belongings. On the table lay the bunch of letters tied with a red ribbon which she had left alone in a hurry. 'Did you see her room?' Greta's mother asked with a smile.

She had changed her clothes. A red chintz skirt and a loose brown cardigan. The room was redolent with the smell of cheap scent.

'This is not tea, but a feast!' I said, looking at the items on the table. Toast, jam, butter, cheese—I don't know when I'd last seen so many things together.

'I got these from a hospital canteen—they are cheap there.'

She looked worried. She laughed, but traces of the worry remained. I wondered where the child was. She was yelling for her and the tea was getting cold.

She sat holding her head in her hands. Suddenly she remembered I was also there.

'Carry on, please. She must be in the garden.'

'You have a garden of your own?' I asked.

'A tiny one, at the back of the kitchen. It was a derelict piece of waste when we came here. My husband cleared it. And now it's producing some vegetables.'

'Your husband doesn't live here?'

'He did not get a job here—he would wander all day in the park. Greta has picked up the same habit.'

There was a slight weariness in her voice. Devoid of any annoyance of course—but a weariness nevertheless, which settles like dust on everything.

'Well, I too lounge about in the park,' I said airily, wanting to make her smile a bit. And I did. She laughed.

'You are different,' she said, 'you are alone. But with a family it is impossible to live in London without a job.'

She began to clear the table. I gathered the utensils in a heap and carried them to the kitchen. A window against the sink looked out into their garden. A weeping willow stood in the centre, its branches swinging like the spokes of an inverted umbrella.

I saw her as I turned. She stood at the door, a towel in her hand.

'What are you looking at?'

'Your garden...it is not that small.'

'It's not...but the tree has grabbed the entire space. I wanted to fell it, but she became adamant—and spent the night crying.'

She fell silent—as though the recollection of that night was a matter of profound grief in itself.

'What did she say?'

'What could she say...she simply wouldn't let me do it. Long ago her father may possibly have told her that they'd build a summer-house under the tree—now you tell me, how can we make a summer-house for dolls in the garden when we don't have enough room for ourselves?'

'A summer-house?'

'Yes, a summer-house—where Greta would live with her bear.'

She started laughing—a sad, melancholic laughter that rose from a void and ended up in another void, leaving the intermediate space also empty.

It was time for me to leave, but Greta did not appear. We went up the stairs. The murky sunlight of London was slithering up the neighbouring chimneys.

As I held out my hand to take leave, she said with some hesitation, 'Are you free tomorrow?'

'Well, I am free almost every day.'

'It is Sunday tomorrow,' she said, 'Greta has a holiday, but I have to go to the hospital. May I leave her with you?'

'When should I come?'

'No, please don't bother. I'll leave her in front of the library on my way to the hospital and take her back when I return later in the evening.'

I nodded and stepped out onto the street. After I had walked some distance, I took out the money from my pocket and began to count it. I was happy I'd saved on dinner. I pressed the small change in my fist and walked homewards.

I was standing at the door of the library. They were late—perhaps due to the cold. In the absence of the sun a faintly discernible patina of light covered the buildings of London—a pale, yellow light that made them look even more derelict and sad.

I caught a glimpse of her white uniform. They were both coming through the park. She in front and Greta running behind her. She waved as she saw me, gave Greta a swift kiss and hastened towards the hospital.

But there was no sign of hurry in the child. She took her time coming to me. Her nose was scarlet in the cold. She wore a full-sleeved brown sweater and on her head the same old cap that I'd seen so often in the park.

She stood there, looking exhausted.

'Coming?' I took her hand.

She nodded quietly. I was slightly dismayed. I had thought that she would at least ask, 'Where?' But she asked me nothing and we set out to cross the road.

She looked questioningly at me as we left the park behind us: for her it was like going out of her charmed circle. But I told her nothing and she did not pursue her mute inquiry. I realized then that when children are not with their parents, they make a parcel of all their queries and throw it in some dark hole.

She looked somewhat reassured as we got into the tube. She left my hand and began to look out of the window.

'Is it night already?' she asked.

'Why night?'

'Look, it is so dark outside.'

'We are underground,' I said.

She mused, then said softly, 'It's night below, and day above.'

Both of us laughed. This had never struck me before.

Gradually we saw the light. A patch of sky first and then the day, bathed in endless sheets of white, hurtled toward us as we came out of the tunnel.

She stopped while climbing the stairs of the tube station. I looked at her in surprise.

'What's the matter?'

'I must go to the bathroom.'

She stood, her hands between her legs, looking as if she were on the verge of a crisis.

I shuddered. The toilet was downstairs and it was doubtful whether she could have walked that far without making a mess. I lifted her and rushed back down the staircase. The toilet—for gents—was at the other end of the corridor and I hustled her in. When I closed the door behind me I felt a tremendous surge of relief.

She looked perturbed as she came out. 'What's it now?'

'The chain is too high,' she said.

'Wait here, I'll pull it.'

She hung onto my coat. She wanted to pull it herself. I went in with her, picked her up and raised her high until the chain was within her reach. We watched the water gushing down the toilet with wonder, as if witnessing this miracle for the first time.

We climbed the steps a second time. She held my hand tightly when we reached the top. Trafalgar Square lay before us, crowded, bright and noisy. I wanted to give her a surprise. But she was frightened. She was so frightened that I almost led her back to the tube station, where the earth contained a secure darkness.

But soon her fright melted away and after a while she released my hand. She was lost in the marvelous light of the square. She ducked under the 'lions' who started intently at the passing crowd—their claws splayed out on the black stones. A number of children were feeding corn to the pigeons. The shadows of their wings looked like clouds carried by the air currents to different directions. Passing over the head, they'd leave behind a hot, sharp flutter in the ears.

She was listening. She'd forgotten me.

I sneaked past her to the centre of the square. There was a cabin made of redwood—where corn was sold for four pence a cup. I bought a cup and searched for her in the crowd.

There were many children surrounded by the pigeons. But she stood where she was. She had not budged an inch from her place. I went behind her and held out the cup of corn.

She looked at me with surprise. Children are never grateful—they merely accept. A third eye opens that levels down all silences. She nearly snatched the cup from my hand and asked, 'Will they come?'

'They'll certainly come...you'll first have to throw the grains one by one to tempt them to come, and then...'

She didn't hear me. She ran in the direction where a couple of pigeons hovered absently. In the beginning, she stretched out her palm rather timidly. The pigeons hesitated—as if her timidity had touched them too. But they couldn't restrain themselves for long. Abandoning their gimmicks, they came closer—feigning indifference, a look here and a look there—and began to pick the grain briskly from her palm. She was now sitting down with her frock spread on the ground. The cup in one hand and corn in the other. She was out of my sight now, the grey fluttering ceiling of wings had canopied her from view.

I sat down on the bench and watched the fountains whose water came flying up to my knees in haphazard drops. The clouds hung so low that the head of Nelson looked like a black speck.

The day wore on.

After a while I found her standing before me.

'I'd like to have one more cup,' she said.

'No more, now,' I said with some hesitation. 'It's quite late. We'll have tea—and you'll have an ice-cream.'

She shook her head.

'I'll have one more cup.'

There was no obstinacy in that tone. As though it was the intimacy which had developed a few moments before which was urging, not me, but her.

I took the empty cup from her and started for the shop. I looked back, she was watching me. I went behind the shop. It was crowded and her eyes could not reach me. Slipping into a corner, I took out the change from my pocket. I put aside some money for tea and ice-cream and for the tube; I was left with only two pence. I added some money from the tea fund and queued up in front of the shop.

This time when I gave her the cup she didn't even glance at me. She ran off immediately to the spot where there was the largest cluster of pigeons. Now her spirits were high. And the pigeons had also started to recognize her. Flying around, they'd perch now on her hand, now on her shoulder, and now on her head. She laughed unceasingly, her pale face almost distorted with a feverish strain. And her hands, those hands which had always seemed so helpless to me, opened and closed with a strange restlessness, as if they'd grab the fluttering, fleshy throbs of the pigeons any moment. She did not know when the cup emptied. She continued to sit for some time, her palms stretched out in the air. Suddenly she realized that the pigeons had left her and were now flocking to the other children. She got up and, without looking in any direction, walked towards me.

'We shall go now,' I got up from the bench.

'I'll have one more cup.'

'No, not any more—you have had two.' I was annoyed. 'You know how much money we are left with?'

'Just one, and then we'll go home.'

People were staring at us. I was arguing over a bowl of corn. I picked her up and sat her on the bench. 'Greta, you're so obstinate. Now you won't get anything.'

She looked at me coldly.

'You are a bad man. I'll never play with you.' I felt she was comparing me to some invisible person. I sat down, feeling empty. There are times when there seems to be no hope for oneself. Only an extreme bewilderment at one's being—one is bewildered because one is. Then I heard a sound which I hear even now in solitude and turned my face.

She was crying. The empty cup was in her hand. And her cap was askew on her forehead. It was a lament in silence. I couldn't bear it. I took the cup from her hand and walked off to join the queue. This time I did not even think of counting the change. I heard only her sobs though she was quite a distance from me. Moreover, the flutter of pigeons and the screams of the children drowned out every other sound. Yet above and beyond all this was a dreadful quiescence within me, holding in its centre her choked breathing—and this I could hear from an endless distance.

But this time there was a difference. For a long while, no pigeon came near her. They'd come close, but perhaps because of her mounting nervousness, or perhaps, again, because of the gathering dusk, they'd fly away to the other children, ignoring her open palm. In desperation she left the cup on the ground and came away to sit by me.

A flock of pigeons flew to the cup as soon as she had left. After a while we noticed that the cup lay careened, empty of grain.

'Will you come now?' I said.

Immediately she got up, as if she had been waiting only to be asked. Her eyes gleamed—a wet gleam, which comes after the tears.

Those days there used to be a Lyons Restaurant in front of the square. It was both dirty and cheap. We crossed the street and went in.

In the meantime I had counted the change in my pocket. I ordered two toasts for her and a cup of tea for myself. It was best to forget about the ice-cream.

This was her first visit to a restaurant. She looked around, deeply curious. I felt that the anguish of the past few moments was melting away. We were again close to each other. But not with the same intensity—the shadow of the pigeons still fluttered between us.

'Am I such a bad man?' I asked.

She lifted her eyes, watched me for a moment, and then said rather anxiously. 'I hadn't meant you.'

'Not me?' I looked at her, baffled. 'Then whom did you say that to?'

'Mr Thomas—he's a bad man. One day when I had gone to their house, he was yelling—and poor Mrs Thomas was crying.'

'Oh!' I said.

'And you thought—I had said that to you?'

She began to laugh, as if I had committed a fatuous blunder. And, I don't know why, my heart sank when I saw her laugh.

'Shall we come here again?' she said.

'In summer,' I said. 'We will go to the Thames which is not far from here.'

'Will there be pigeons there?' she asked.

So like a girl's repeated reference to her lover, that hurt me. But I hated to disappoint her again. The summer was far away, we had still to go through autumn and the days of snow—by then my life would also melt away, I thought.

Although the afternoon was not yet over, there were traces of dusk in its maw when we emerged from the restaurant. She looked absently at the square, where the pigeons were still flying. I had money barely enough to scramble home in the tube. Mercifully, she made no demands. I have a feeling that, beyond a certain limit, children are able to sense the misery, if not the poverty, of grown-ups.

I had thought I would ask her about the summerhouse when we boarded the tube—and about the willow which stood majestically alone in her garden. I wanted to bring her back to her own world—where we had first met one another. But this did not happen. Her eyes grew heavy almost as soon as she sat down. It was quite a distance from Trafalgar Square to Islington. After a few moments, she leaned her head against my shoulder and fell asleep.

I briefly studied her face. I was amazed to see that she looked the same as I had seen her first, among the trees in the park—absorbed and intact. The restlessness that had surfaced with the pigeons was no more. Her tears had long dried up. In sleep she looked as secure as she did in the bushes. And then an odd thought came to my mind. She had ensnared me a number of times in the park. But looking at her intense face I felt that while people like me are caught rarely, here was a girl who had always been trapped. She was not aware of it, which was fortunate because the adult is always under the illusion of being set free, of being released, while the child has no such hope. Then for the first time I had the courage to caress her. I touched her cheeks warm after tears, but she slept.

The rain, which started on that night, continued for a week. The days of a false summer were over. The city lay shrouded in layers of a pale mist. One could see nothing while walking on the road—the trees, lamp posts, or the people. I remember those days because that was the time I had found a job. It was my first job in London. The load of work was heavy, though not tough. I had to stand at the counter of a pub for seven hours. I had to clean the glasses of beer and spirits. I had to ring the bell at eleven and drive out the drunkards. I could not go anywhere for some days. I'd return home and take to bed, as though sleep would resolve an old feud. Whenever I opened my eyes I saw the rain which like the incessant ticking of a watch, continued without respite. Sometimes I had a feeling that I was dead and listening from the other end of my grave to the pattern of falling rain.

But one day I saw the sky, not all of it, but just a blue, sunken slice—and suddenly memories of the days in the park, of the cat in the Jewish restaurant and of Mrs Thomas on her way to the market, flooded back. It was a holiday. I put on my best clothes and got out of the room.

The library was open. All the old faces were there. The park was empty. The rain of the previous days glistened on the trees. They looked somewhat shrunken, as if the rumour of the impending winter had touched them too.

I waited till the afternoon. Greta was nowhere to be seen, either on the bench or behind the trees. The pale, autumnal glow in the park was fading out. The hospital clock struck five and my eyes involuntarily turned towards the gate.

The last rays of the evening lit up the iron handle on the gate. And the red-brick hospital building loomed large behind it. I knew that she had to walk through the park to get home, and yet my eyes wandered uncertainly from the gate to the road. I also thought that perhaps it was her day off and they might both be home.

The street lights came on. I felt strangely nervous, as if the end of the waiting had arrived and I was avoiding it. I stood up from the bench—it seemed easier to wait standing up. But just then I heard a movement near the gate. I spotted her uniform even before I saw her face. She was walking briskly along the footpath in the middle of the park. She had not noticed me. Even if she were to come in my direction, she would perhaps not have recognized me in the twilight.

I ran behind her.

'Mrs Parker.' It was the first time I had addressed her by name.

She stopped, momentarily taken aback when she saw me. She had recognized me, but seemed unable to grasp the meaning of this recognition. I felt a bit awkward and said in a normal voice, 'You are returning rather late today. It's long past five.'

'Five?' she asked in surprise.

'You always returned at five,' I said.

'Oh!' she recalled, as if I was talking of some pre-historic time. 'Were you in London all these days?' she asked.

'I've found a job. And that kept me away. How is Greta?'

She hesitated—a tiny moment's hesitation which had no significance, but in the evening haze it seemed sinister.

'I wanted to tell you, but I did not know where you lived.'

'Is she all right?'

'Yes, she's all right,' she said swiftly, 'but she is not here now. Her father had come a few days back to fetch her. She has gone with him.'

I was looking at her. Everything within me ground to a halt—I was within it, within that stillness, and the world stood without. I had never seen the outside with such clarity.

'When was it?'

'The day you had taken her to Trafalgar Square. He came the day after that...you know he has found a job there.'

'And you?' I asked. 'You'll live here all alone?'

'I haven't made up my mind yet.' She lifted her head, her voice quivered and momentarily I caught a glimpse of the girl in her face: the turned lips and wet eyes, watching the pigeons flutter in the air.

'You must come to our house some day.' She wanted to take leave and I stretched out my hand. I followed her with my eyes for a long distance. Then I sat down on the bench. I had nowhere to go, nor reason to wait. Slowly the stars appeared over the trees. It was the first time I had seen so many stars in the London sky, calm and bright, as if the rains had washed them too.

'It is time dear!'

The watchman of the park called out from a distance. He was going around the park, clattering the keys of the gate, checking under each tree, bush and bench with his torch for stragglers—a lost child, a drunkard, or a domestic cat.

There was no one there. Nothing had been left behind. I got up and moved towards the gate. Suddenly the wind picked up. A light breeze strayed into the darkness and the trees rustled. And then I heard a feeble voice, full of insistence. 'Stop...stop.' My feet came to a sudden halt in the middle of the park. I looked about. No one. No sound. No warning...only the trees swayed in the wind. And suddenly I was overcome by an almost frenzied, desperate urge to sit there. Amidst the trees where I had been caught the first time. I did not wish to go any further. I wanted to be caught, finally and irrevocably.

'It is closing time!' the watchman called, coming closer. He looked curiously at me, wondering if I was the same man who had been sitting on the bench a while go.

This time I did not turn. And breathed only after I had got out of the park. My throat was parched. It was nice to see the lantern of the pub opposite the park. I took out my wallet to count the money. The habits of penury die hard. I was astonished to see that I still had two pounds—and then I remembered, I had brought this much money for the pigeon-corn.

A Night in London

London Ki Ek Raat

I had gone there for the second time. The previous night I was late. Workers had been hired even before I reached. I hung around uncertainly by the gate. There was a faint hope that they might need someone at the last minute. I could hear the sound of the bottles above the hum of the machines and I could see those who had been hired changing into overalls.

Outside in the courtyard, the bottles, gleaming in the moonlight, stood one upon the other, in neat rows, close to the factory wall.

I continued to wait. After a while an Englishman came to me.

'You still here? Didn't I tell you there wasn't anything going today,' he said and laid his hand on my shoulder.

'I was just looking on,' I said, relieving my shoulder gently from his grip.

'You come tomorrow 15 minutes early. We'll take you on if some of them don't turn up. Good Night.'

Today was my second night. As I climbed up from the tube station, I found the moon in full bloom. The smoky London sky was shriveled up among the many chimneys. For the second time I was groping my way here along the same streets I had walked yesterday—streets which were known to me now and yet appeared strangely unfamiliar in the moonlight.

A few steps beyond North Acton, my feet refused to budge. I am early today, I had thought, and there would be no one at the gate except myself. But I was wrong. There was already a crowd of unemployed young men gathered there. About 20 to 25: some English boys, a few students who looked Burmese, Negroes from South Africa and the West Indies—they were all standing in separate little groups. All of them had their eyes on the gate. Some of the faces looked familiar. Maybe I had seen them the previous night. Their eyes slid up to me, tense and unspeaking. Their silence roused a strange fear within me in some way linked with an unknown destiny, which was going to be decided in the next few moments. This was our bond. I stood along with them in a corner, fearing them, and yet beholden to them.

Around a quarter to nine the manager appeared. He was not the same man who had put his hand on my shoulder yesterday. He held a slip in his hand. All of us silently moved closer to him like the animals in a zoo clambering to the bars of their cage in the hope of getting something. He gave us a quick glance. He must have been slightly frightened by our open, bare, expressionless faces, for he quickly lowered his eyes to the paper in his hand and began reading out names.

All those who had worked earlier were taken. Besides them, only three other boys were called—two English boys who looked like vagabonds and one student from South Africa who had been standing in front and leaning forward to whisper now and then into the ear of the manager.

'That'll be all for today,' he looked sympathetically at us. 'Please come tomorrow. We might need you'.

Three or four boys moved forward from the crowd to argue, but he raised his hands in a gesture of helplessness and turned away, his eyes smiling at us.

We knew there was nothing more to wait for, yet we couldn't quite believe it. Although the manager was gone, none of us budged from where we stood. It seemed as though the scene of the last three minutes was not over yet—in some way unreal, little to do with us... (there is something in us which keeps the doors ajar even after the wait). There were many among us who had spent three to four shillings to get here from distant corners of London. We each carried a bag in which were our overalls and a snack. That we must now return by the next tube was difficult for us to take. The lukewarm water dripping from the tap, the muddy pools gleaming in the moonlight—even the empty bottle lying in the gutter seemed a little ludicrous... Perhaps we had even forgotten why we were here. Our disappointment over missing the job a few minutes ago, now clung to our legs like an ugly burden that we had to drag home with us.

At that moment there was no trace of irritation or bitterness in us, in spite of the hunger and the disappointment. It didn't last, though. Suddenly the uncanny moment was shattered. We were back in ourselves. The odour of each other's bodies—which we could smell standing so close, and own up, despite the abuses—began to disperse in different directions. Only three of us were left standing uncertainly in the courtyard. I heard a faint rustle behind me.

'Bloody bastard!' One of the men muttered in a gruff, low voice. He moved forward, took a frightened look around and picking up a bottle of soda from the dozens of crates, began to drink from it. 'Drink it, chum. Them bastards won't even know,' he said thrusting a bottle into the hands of the other man.

The other man, who looked a teenaged Negro student, hesitated, but after some thought and a jerk of his head, he grabbed the bottle with both his hands like a child, and raised it to his lips. He took a large draught, wiped his face on his bare arm and held out the bottle to me.

'This is the third time I have come here. The guy who promised me a job yesterday is nowhere to be seen today,' he said.

'It will be the same tomorrow. Some other bastard will appear and he won't even know we have been here tonight.'

'But who's coming to this place tomorrow anyway! I won't look this way. Damn them, these...'

The first man unbuttoned his overcoat. Even in this heat he had an overcoat on. But it didn't surprise me. The man seemed inseparable from it. If he hadn't had an overcoat I would have been surprised. He was a tall, heavily built youth, who sported a small blonde beard, had eyes blinking from behind the beard in a dry, bitter perplexity. No, not perplexity really, but a queer, nervous strain one usually sees in hunted animals. With his figure of a Hollywood villain he could be frightening to a stranger in the dark.

We were walking slowly. We had reached North Acton Bridge. A London double-decker drove past with a trail of crisp yellow leaves of August chasing it. The Negro youth was still dejected. He walked quietly, his eyes lowered to the street. 'How long have you been in London?' the bearded youth (who later gave his name as Willie) asked the Negro, putting his hand on his shoulder.

The Negro didn't answer.

'Where are you from?'

'South Africa. I study here.'

Perhaps he wanted the matter to end there. He pulled out a packet of cigarettes from his pocket and held it before us. We thanked him and turned our eyes away. It was his last cigarette and we weren't going to take it. But this formality did not last and a few moments later we were taking turns at the lighted cigarette.

Above us was the wearying London sky—grimy and calm. This was a desolate corner of the city and the street was empty—empty, but not abandoned. The rustling of leaves, the stale smell of old houses (we seemed to be wading through a host of lifeless objects) and nothing else except the wind and the rings around the lamp-posts...

'Where do you go?'

'Warren Street,' he said. 'Been coming here two days now. Five shillings wasted on the journey alone. I could have gone for tennis instead.'

Tennis! That sounded odd. From his face you got the impression he hadn't had enough to eat for days.

'My friend has work,' the Negro was saying, somewhat zealously. 'We live together. He might lend me a few shillings tomorrow.'

'Damn him, if he doesn't!' Willie exclaimed in a strange, peevish tone. 'I'm not coming here tomorrow. Please come tomorrow, be damned. Will you be coming?' he was asking me, talking directly to me for the first time. 'Maybe, yes,' I said deliberately to annoy him. His talk about tomorrow at this moment made me sore.

'What do these bastards pay you?'

'Two and a half pounds,' said the Negro.

'Every morning?'

'Yes. Every morning. They also give you tea and sandwiches at midnight, my friend tells me. We had come together yesterday. He was picked up, I was left out.'

'A Negro?'

'No. He's Burmese.'

'And you?' Willie looked sideways at me, as if sizing me up. 'You a Jap?'

I nodded. It seemed pointless to contradict him over a minor matter.

We walked on towards the tube station in silence for a while. Whenever there came a whiff of warm breeze we trembled. Our hunger then broke through all pretences.

'It's quite hot. We've never known such heat during the last five years.'

'Have you been five years in London?'

'Perhaps more. I have done a number of odd stints since. But now I won't stay long.'

'Will you return home?' Willie asked.

'Home?' he demanded as if he had heard the word for the first time. 'I wanted to live here. But they don't want us.'

'They... ah!' said Willie. Suddenly we looked about. There was no one there, although 'they' were always with us, everywhere. Outside, as much as within...

'Were you here when there was a riot in Jarring Hill?' asked the Negro. Willie's white teeth glistened.

'No, I hadn't yet arrived,' I said.

'I live there. I hid three days in the house of an English girl. When they were lynching every Negro they could get hold of, I was screwing that white whore. She thought I liked her... but I didn't so much as see her afterwards. She doesn't know I was seeking revenge... upon her white skin...'. And he made a sign with his hand which was more repelling than obscene.

Far away, beyond the smoke of the factories, the lights of the tube station were agleam as though a patch of earth had broken into two and a frill of glittering diamonds emerged from under it.

'Do you study here?'

'Yes, but I work in the summer vacations. Earlier I used to go out to dances,' said George. His voice was sad, as if the pain of missing the job still persisted.

'Why don't you push off to the continent, buddy?' said Willie. 'A friend of mine has gone to Germany. There is no dearth of jobs there. They say the girls there are crazy about black colour. You just have to signal.'

'Maybe, because of the last war,' said George. 'Some years ago my father was there. He used to say you couldn't find a man there. Only women all around.'

'Oh, how I long for another war... another and then another,' said Willie.

George looked at Willie in surprise and then at me. Perhaps he wanted to say something, but then he changed his mind and he simply nodded. And, perhaps, it was the right thing to do. In that hot night in London, 'war' seemed too distant... senseless and ludicrous. It wasn't worth arguing over. And that's what happened. We soon forgot about 'war' and went on talking for a long time about girls in different countries. And so out of the old one a new hunger grew.

'I wanted to go to Spain. The girls there... ah! Passion. But the bastards wouldn't give me the visa. They seem rather particular about their girls there!'

'Spain...' It was as though someone had poked smouldering embers...

'Have you been there?'

'I wanted to, long ago.'

'During the Civil War?'

'I was too young then.'

'Civil war in our country... perhaps,' and suddenly George fell silent. Beads of perspiration gleamed on his curly hair.

'I don't like the civil war,' said Willie.

Talk had again got stuck at the same point, like the bead of the bagatelle that gets stuck again and again at the same hole at the end of each round. We had nothing to do with it. It was a very calm and hot night, and war seemed too distant a thing.

'Come, let's have some beer. I can't sleep well unless I've had a drink,' said Willie.

I was in two minds. I had my last two shillings in my pocket and I had kept them for the tube. George did not look very eager either. He was whistling in the dark, half-listening to Willie's proposal.

Perhaps Willie understood. He put a hand on George's shoulder and said, 'There's nothing to worry about. People here know me. I used to frequent this place.'

George's sullenness vanished all of a sudden. A strange, childish joy glowed in his face.

'I will have only gin. I hope my friend will lend me a few shillings tomorrow.'

We walked to the pub. A hot, simmering wave of voices swept over us as we opened the door—voices intertwining, merging, jostling each other in the smoke, gathered in a pool, spilling over itself. The lights were dim, encircled by clouds of smoke in which it was impossible to tell one face from another.

Down a flight of stairs was the basement. Shadows of dancing couples moved across the staircase—long and formless at times, and at others, tiny shadows like that of fish moving under clear water.

We sat down at a corner table. Moments later, Willie fetched three bottles of beer and glasses.

'I used to work here. Got fed up after some months of it. The owner of this pub is an Italian. Not a bad man, but very timid. I'll introduce you if he comes along,' Willie said.

'Must have earned fat tips here?'

'The English don't give much. Half a shilling at best. But it's another thing with tourists from the continent. They are open-hearted, and also very foolish.'

'I'd pick up anything I got,' George said. The beer had untied the knots inside us. There were wings now, flapping to fly.

'I won't stay in this land very long,' Willie was saying. 'My friend is in Germany. If possible, I will go there one of these days.'

He finished his glass and turned it over on the table. There wasn't a drop left to spill. His beard was stuck with froth, wet and white like grains of sand.

'I can't stand the Germans,' George said.

'Life is real there. There are young girls, standing in every corner,' cooed Willie.

'I can't stand the Germans,' repeated George.

I began to laugh. George turned his eyes on me. His eyes looked wretched.

'They are all alike,' said Willie.

'But those people...' George pointed outwards, out of the door, out into the dark.

'Even they. You are just scared,' said Willie.

George's hand, resting on his glass quivered a little.

'You are a rotter,' he said.

There must have been something in his voice, for Willie's face grew pale at once.

'Watch out. I can get really nasty. Don't you say that again.'

'Oh! Really?' George's voice seemed to make a tightrope, as if it would plunge into the abyss any moment. 'You are a rotter,' he repeated.

In no time Willie had leapt to his feet, glass in hand. But the action looked more like a game he was used to playing, so he must stand up according to the rules. 'Repeat that!'

His glass was now close to George's head. Some froth from the beer in it caught the light and gleamed. George lifted his face with his eyes half-closed to him.

'Yes, you are a rotter all the same,' he said. Under the glass, the Negro's head shook. It seemed quite ridiculous to me that a human head should tremble so on its own axis, independent of the rest of the body.

Willie looked at him, astonished, and then burst into laughter.

'Maybe you're right... Maybe I am...'. He sank into his chair. We had not drunk much. But, we felt trapped.

After some time the owner of the pub came and stood by our table. He was rotund, well-built, and more yellow than fair. His hair was dark, curly, soaked in oil and stuck to his small forehead.

'Care for more?' he smiled, looking at Willie.

'It's here... Later on, maybe,' Willie said. His voice was no longer tense, but it did not conceal a note of disdain. 'These,' he said, 'are my friends.'

The Italian's eyes swept over us without curiosity.

'Willie has worked with us,' he looked proudly at Willie.

'Been long here?' he asked.

George was silent. It was a relief his head did not tremble any more. I was fidgeting with the empty glass and my hands stopped still.

'Only a few days,' I said.

'Isn't it nice?' he asked.

'Any job?' he was staring at my shirt-collar. It had layers of dirt on it—I don't know from how many countries.

'Nothing at the moment.'

'Willie can get work but he won't stick to it.' There was affection and reproach in his eyes as he looked at Willie.

'I could have stayed with you, but you...'

Suddenly the Italian's face clouded with grief. 'You know...' he began.

'Ah,' said Willie. 'You are all alike.'

'It's so hot,' George muttered, as if in an aside.

'No, I don't know anything. I know only that I will dance now.'

Willie pushed back his chair and got up. But the Italian held him by the shoulder. His eyes looked terrified. His short, ball-like body looked wretched against Willie's tall, spare frame.

'Willie. You know, here...'.

Willie shrugged the hand off his shoulder. Now he had his back to our table. George grabbed the beer bottle. For a moment it appeared as if we were sitting in a tossing deck.

As the orchestra began to play, pairs of girls and boys from the corners of the pub began descending the basement stairs. The Italian did not even look back. He kept gazing into the air in front.

Willie had disappeared.

His empty glass was lying on our table. George eased his grip round the bottle. The sweat on his palm had left a white mark. The Italian looked in our direction, as if unable to recognize us. Then, he threw up his hands.

'He's crazy... isn't he?' he said.

We kept quiet. There certainly was something, precisely at this moment, which, though not concerned directly with us, had spread its shadow stealthily between us. With heavy, weary steps, he turned to the counter.

'It's so hot,' said George. 'How much money do you have on you?'

'Why?' Suddenly everybody seemed to annoy me.

'I've got a shilling and a half. Can you buy a lager with that?' he asked.

I was watching Willie's empty glass.

'Where could he be?'

'Perhaps he got annoyed... I couldn't restrain myself,' said George.

'You haven't said anything to him?'

'I can't restrain myself,' he clasped my hand, which was lying on the table. My fingers under his palm grew clammy.

'You don't know... I am very fond of boxing. When I first arrived in London and was not jobless, I went boxing every day. But I haven't won, even once, till now... There is something the matter with me. A strange kind of tension growing in me. I wait, for long moments, for the other person to hit first...and when he doesn't, I feel uncontrollably roused. I can't wait with the possibility of an attack still threatening. I jump the gun and charge. I charge blindly. I know it's wrong, it's not the way to fight. And that's why I ran away from home. I can't wait like my father.'

'And he? What's he waiting for?'

'I don't know... I have no interest in politics.' His forehead hid behind the glass of lager.

Gently I freed my hand. It was covered with sweat. I lifted it close to myself as if it were a little pet animal—a lump of white flesh, entwined with very pale brown fingers, too much of hair growing all over, still crumpled from his touch. And, I thought, we seldom look at our hands in this way—the way they really are—and then suddenly you realize you could never claim as your own a thing once it has fallen into the grip of those hands.

'You know why I called Willie a rotter?'

'That was nothing,' I said but couldn't look him in the eye.

'Why, I am myself one. I told you just now that I hold my father in great esteem.' (He had never told me any such thing.) 'You don't know him. I don't know if he is alive or not. They were after his blood.'

'They? Who?'

'They...' A great cold horror settled in his eyes like a coiled snake, 'You've never seen.'

He gripped my hand with a vehemence. His black face showed only his white teeth with his lips drawn from one ear to the other, and I couldn't decide whether he was laughing or whether it was just his teeth showing in a moment of forgetfulness.

'I am safe here, and I hate him like hell for that.'

We drank on in silence. For the first time I noticed the face of a clock on the wall in front of me. I felt an urge to smoke. It seemed I hadn't smoked for a long, long time.

'What do you think?'

There was a childlike insistence in his voice.

'Nothing.'

'What would you've done in my place?'

'In your place?' I laughed. 'I don't even know what I ought to do in my own place!'

'But surely you must have decided before you left your country.'

'Perhaps escape?'

'Escape? From what?'

'From my countrymen. Perhaps from other things, too, which I can't recollect just now.'

And at that moment I felt that perhaps it was not possible to drink any more. I hadn't eaten anything since morning. The lager filled my empty intestines. A purple mist had gathered inside the restaurant at each of the windows from where I could have looked out. There was the face of the clock... very white... like an ancient corpse swaying in the air...

'Why are you grinning?'

I was surprised to know that I had been grinning and, once I knew I had been grinning, it looked silly to restrain laughter.

'What is it?' he asked.

'Nothing. I just recalled something,' I said evasively.

'What did you recall?' He leaned over towards me as if to hang by my throat. 'Tell me, what did you recall?'

'Do you know... I would have landed in jail only three days ago. I escaped by the skin of my teeth.'

How odd that one can recall something or the other even under extreme stress! And I really remembered an incident which took place three days before.

'Yes. I escaped by the skin of my teeth.' (I am fond of such expressions and I keep repeating them in or out of season.)

'You know, I stay with a friend here in London. For the last few days, he has had his girlfriend from Finland, too. There's just one room; so I am keeping out. During the day I wander around the museum library, and at night I go over to the Euston station to sleep. Every day at an appointed time my friend comes round and hands me a few shillings. That evening he couldn't come for some reason and I was left with just ten pence. The whole day I didn't notice that I was hungry; for I was in the museum, but later I could hardly bear it. By then, the cheap eating places at King's Cross were closed and I couldn't afford a bus ride to the centre of the city. I was wandering about Warren Street station for a long time in bewilderment. Finally I caught sight of a Greek joint which appeared quite cheap. I went in and ordered potato chips and toast and sat down. You know these things are the cheapest—eight pence at the most. I was quite confident. After a few moments, my eyes suddenly fell on the price list on the wall in front of me which I had overlooked in my nervousness. Toast and chips cost one-and-a-half shillings and I had only the ten pennies... Then, you know what I did? I got to my feet abruptly, like this (and I really stood up before George), and called out, 'Good Evening. Ah, why are you standing outside?' 'I'll be back in a moment,' I said, and rushed to the door, leaving the plate of toast and chips uneaten on the table, with perfectly steady steps, like this (and I really walked between the tables), but no sooner did I cross the door... you know... I didn't look back.' (I came back to George again... I took a large sip of the lager and sat down.) 'I ran on for a long time.'

'And he chased after you?'

'No. That's the joke. He did not chase me and yet I ran from one dark alley to another. And, look, now that my hunger had vanished completely I had saved the ten pennies in my pocket.'

'You are wonderful,' George was laughing. It delighted me to see him laugh.

'My friend and his beloved also laughed when I told them about it. But, it is not surprising that even those who have such experiences, often make light of them! For, you see, when you are in it, you are absolutely miserable, your shirt clinging to your skin, sweat pouring from your sides and your heart filled with a rending wretchedness... In spite of our age. In spite of our experience. I know that... that night, as I ran for my life, down the dark streets, with ten pennies clutched in my fist in the pocket, it kept on ringing in my ears: "You bloody fool, you idiot...you...". '

'You are wonderful,' George said. When he had repeated this for the third time, I just couldn't restrain myself. The face of the clock began to reel before my eyes once again and I stood up and made for the toilet in the basement. Hurriedly I began descending the steps. I was afraid something might happen on the staircase itself. I covered my mouth with my hands and smiled, rather secretively.

Nothing happened—either on the stairs, or at the washbasin over which I leaned for a long time, waiting to throw up. The white dial reeling before my eyes was gone now.

As I emerged from the toilet, my feet seemed to have lost all their motion all of a sudden. I was caught among the whirling, dancing couples. People jostled past me, now turning left, now right, like puppets. Whenever I tried to steady my feet, the floor below seemed to shrink and I felt as if I were standing on a top swooning to a stop. Presently I felt a strange weight upon my shoulders.

'You're here,' Willie's beard pricked my forehead. 'And George?'

'He's there,' I pointed upwards.

The girl he was dancing with had her face hidden in his chest, only her blonde hair showed from time to time.

'Aren't you going?... your lager...' I asked.

'I'll go. Won't you dance?'

This time the girl lifted up her face. There were patches of powder on her bare shoulders and she was wearing a cheap chintz summer skirt. Little beads of sweat from her lips spluttered the lipstick, maybe because she had been dancing long.

It was impossible to remain in the crowd. Willie and the girl dancing close to me, with very slow steps, in a very narrow circle... one moment it was Willie's head near me, the next her blonde hair...

'How is she?'

Willie gave her hair a mild jerk. She was laughing.

'She's just too bad... isn't she?' he told her, laughing, and for the first time I saw that her eyes resembled a shut-eye doll's—as if they would close if she threw back her head, and reopen as soon as she straightened up.

'Would you like to dance? Maybe with her?' Willie said.

They were both circling round and round, with very slow steps. As they came close to me one of them would whisper something in my ear.

'Her comrades are sitting over there. They'd be aflame if they saw her with me,' Willie said.

'Won't you dance? Maybe with me?' the girl whispered.

'The Italian has forbidden...' I told Willie.

'Damn him!' Willie snapped.

Strangely, there seemed to float out of the stale orchestral tune, a vague hint of Mozart's 'Battle Music'—just for a moment—and at that very instant I felt that like a thread, my breath had been entwined by somebody around his finger and was being drawn out.

'Care for a gin? She will pay,' Willie whispered in my ear.

'Maybe with me,' the girl said in the same nonchalant voice.

Before I could reply the crowd of dancing couples had swept them along, far away from me. The next moment they were out of sight.

'Hello!'

Someone had gripped my arm. Turning round, I saw the Italian proprietor of the pub. Perhaps he had rushed to me from some distance. His turned-up sleeves were hanging loose on his arms. He was panting, as if there wasn't enough air there.

'Listen! Is he your friend?'

I shrugged.

'Can't you take him away from here—I mean from this place?'

'Why don't you tell him yourself?' I said.

'I can't. He will never listen to anything I say.'

'But why—why can't he stay here?'

'This place is not fit for him,' he said in an imploring, helpless voice. 'I have warned him several times in the past.'

Again I longed to lie down on the staircase.

'You see, I can't do anything. We met only a few hours ago. You don't believe?'

For a moment I was disgusted with his wretched face. The sight of it made me feel as if I had touched something revoltingly fat and soft. 'I hardly know him. Not even his full name,' I told him, as if to know one's full name was vitally important—as if anything depended upon it.

Suddenly he clasped both my hands. He moved up quite close to me. 'You—you will remain here?'

As I reached my table I found George asleep. His head resting on a corner of the table, his body shriveled up in the chair, the whites of his eyes showing through the half-closed lids, like flecks of cotton. At first I thought he was watching me, but no, it wasn't so. Down the edges of his lips, like a thin line of chalk, spittle had gone dry and white. I wiped it off with my handkerchief so that the others would not notice it.

And, at that moment, for the first time I realized how young he was—how ridiculously young and naïve.

Something very odd crossed my mind. It was my last night at home, just before I left for Europe. Mother was getting up again and again, pretending she wanted water, but she was actually staring at me. It was my last night on the terrace of my home. A night in July, and I had to set out the next day. Babu, my father, was standing by my bed, thinking I was asleep. But I could see everything... Even otherwise, our July nights are very bright... and you can see everything even with your eyes closed...

Suddenly I had an urge to go out of the pub. It was quite easy. First, I would have to get up from my chair, open the door, and then... go out... Simply slip out... that's the thing, I thought... There was saliva again, drooling from his mouth, from his lips down to his chin, where a growth of hair like blue thistles jutted out... Again I wiped his mouth with my handkerchief.

Voices... a delirious scream.

Shadows waddled on the wall of the basement like a terrible nightmare. Sound of chairs being pulled, embarrassed laughter. There was nothing. I could have risen... but there was still some lager in the glass and I couldn't get up... Instead, I felt a peculiar sense of peace within myself. Like an endless flow of dense warm sand. And I held on to it.

Just to slip out, just to...

I shook George with all my strength.

He sat up at once, and looked at me in a stupor, almost like a trained animal who has forgotten his lesson and whose eyes roam about over the onlookers. Then, all at once, his eyes were seized by a strange horror.

'What is the matter?'

'Come... We must leave here.'

'But... just now?'

He did not know. In the hurry I couldn't decide whether I ought to tell him anything or not.

'Did I fall asleep?' he asked. I don't know what he noticed in my face which made him suddenly suspicious.

'What is this uproar about?'

His face now looked exactly as it had looked when we were standing by the gate of the factory, in the dark... The clock now appeared so distant and irrelevant...

'We have to go out... out.'

Outside, the London night was waiting to swallow us up.

'Where is Willie? We can't leave without him.'

'He—he can't come.'

The pub door was flung open. A group of people rushed in.

'There they are'. Coarse abuses... senseless voices... like the buzz of flies.

I seized him by the hand and dragged him.

'I won't go.'

'Don't be crazy.'

'Where are they?'

'They...' Angrily, I forced him to get up. He was standing in front of me. 'Tell me, who's they?' I shook him by the shoulder.

'Speak up, who's they?'

'You are drunk,' he said and jerked himself free.

It's time perhaps. I thought, perhaps, I had drunk too much. This thought came as a great comfort.

'You will stay here?'

'What's it to you?' he said.

'Listen,' I tried to get the chair out from between us.

'You are drunk!'

He shrank from me.

I made to go. He, too, but separately. It looked like the game in which two blindfolded persons grope, hoping to drift apart, but only to run into each other.

Moving towards the door, first one comes across the tables, cigarette stubs, empty glasses and bottles; evening papers lying on the chairs, a broken little tube of lipstick in a corner on the floor—perhaps forgotten by a woman in a hurry—and suddenly it seemed to me that there had been an incident, and all of them had been caught, unprepared, in the whirlwind of the fleeing crowd.

Where is Willie...?

And, this Italian...?

I could think no further. The door opened and I felt that George broke away abruptly from me. At the last moment (or perhaps in the initial moment) I tried to hold him to myself, as if this was in itself... but my head drooped from haziness. The arm which I had stretched out to reach George, went on twisting... Ceiling. No, this is no ceiling... only a bulb swinging... And my arm continued to twist... (Don't let them escape, an absent voice said and then not even that)... And the arm, it was trembling and I could see it trembling... As though it were not my own arm. Someone is twisting it, to the point where it will break apart... In my entire body... No, it's not pain, pain has a limit, beyond which you can't know it any more.

'I say... leave him!'

Is it the Italian's voice? It mildly surprised me. Faces that were leaning over me, were lifted up one by one, but I couldn't see them. Just their warm breath that touched my neck off and on, then not even that.

'Can you get up?'

I looked at my arm. It was lying on the floor... Surprising, that it was still connected to my being.

I sat up mechanically. My hands reached for my cheeks. My cheeks were wet—I couldn't believe that it could be tears.

'Drink something.'

The Italian was fidgeting about me.

'Where is Willie?' I asked.

'They'll kill him... What did I tell you?' His voice quivered in a peculiar way.

'What did you tell?... I can't remember.'

'You know... if you had taken him away with you, nothing would have happened.'

'Nothing would have happened?... But who can say it could have been prevented? I will go now,' I said.

'Where?' The Italian stood against the door.

'Anywhere... out.'

I looked about. There was no trace of George. I began to feel vaguely happy.

'Out?'

Perhaps the Italian could not believe his ears. Perhaps he wasn't sure how far he could take me seriously.

'Not now... they are standing outside,' he added.

'Listen,' I said very simply. I'll do nothing. I will go home straight.'

'What do you mean?' This time he suddenly flared up. 'They know you've come with Willie... you can't escape them.'

It was no use arguing.

Outside, the commotion had suddenly increased... I felt a cold twitching crawl up my back for a moment. Cold as ice. I recognized this. It was the beginning of fear. I felt I was grinning.

'Look... Can you give me a small whisky?'

He gazed at me for a few moments. I had crawled forward. Our faces were so close that I could hear him breathing in spite of the uproar outside.

'You won't leave?' His voice was strained with doubt and uncertainty.

'I'm not crazy.'

He gazed silently at me.

'I can't go leaving you here,' he said.

All of a sudden I had an impulse to tear his plump, sweaty face to pieces... but I went on smiling as before.

'I'll stay here for the whisky if not for you. Surely you trust me for that?'

This time his lips were wide with an unexpected grin. There was a desperate helplessness lurking in it as if he were convincing himself that he could trust me.

He advanced towards the counter where the bottles of wine and beer were kept. Now and then he looked back over his shoulder.

I remained standing.

He placed a bottle of Scotch on the counter. He then looked at me as if there were some secret agreement between us.

Our silence seemed louder than the sounds that kept pouring in like waves—intertwined, crashing against the door, and then disappearing in the endless dark.

He was washing a glass. Water flowing from the tap... and its drops racing down the shining glass... I watched the drops and all the while I felt like vomiting... I couldn't stand the sight of water flowing down an empty glass... I took a step towards the door. He still had his back towards me. The gurgling tap-water drowned the sound of my heartbeats... and all of a sudden I felt I couldn't turn even if I tried to—as though I had lost all control over myself... as though I were independent of myself.

The door opened and the next moment I was out, in the dark!

Just to be out—I said to myself.

It was a soft, open summer night, quiet, like a huge wild beast, lying full length in its lair.

The sweat was drying up. I heaved a full sigh—once... twice. There was a nagging sense of regret... I had foregone the whisky... I wished I had it inside me at this moment. Once again I took a deep breath. If only I could have smoked a cigarette! ...Crossing a wide road—I was out into a narrow street... Usually there are auto-machines for cigarettes at street corners.

'Here he is! The son of a bitch!'

I stopped short... No, it was not fear. I was quite calm... only, there was something cold sliding down my spine...

There they were. Shadows clinging to the wall moved forward.

'Hold him!' There was a shriek—and my whole body was suddenly twisted backwards. A whiff of breeze passed through my armpits.

'Goddamned nigger!'

'Wait. Just wait.'

He had come up from behind me. There was no time even to notice that my head was already drawn backwards. Another moment, and I would split into two.

I wished I could see his face!

There was the hand. I could hear the blood pounding at my temples. I stirred a little and crawled forward, dragging him along. But it was some other man—he had only my arms in his grip.

For a moment I was struck with astonishment. Is this my body—quivering like this!

'You shitting swine!'

I tried to free myself with a jerk, but my hair... my hair was caught in his hands and I could see his hairy arm coming over my mouth... and suddenly I plunged my teeth into it... 'Oh, let go, you bugger!' He shook me. Once, twice... but I clung to his arm, like a drunkard.

Was it Willie's voice? I tried to scream with all my strength... nothing but a terrible whirring sound came out.

Then suddenly I felt his grip slacken. I could now lift myself up. My eyes were open. A blue river of gloom flowed out. Red, green and pink patches floating in the horizon. I had been there before, a long, long time ago. A familiar hallucination! I was reviving all over.

At a distance of two yards from me he was standing, stuck to the wall. For a moment I couldn't believe it was Willie, the man I had been drinking lager with only a while ago.

But, could he recognize me?

And that blonde...and George?... Had they all got lost or drowned in the night, beyond the pale of memory?

Only two yards, and the intervening darkness.

A mob, half a face, and a tall young man leaning over Willie... He seized Willie by his collar and dragged him to the other wall... Bang... Bang... The scarf puffed up... The colourful scarf the tall man had worn round his own neck... there were roses printed on it—

Roses... and blood, dripping from Willie's lips to his goatee.

In a flash, everything intermeshed—voices, perspiration, the acrid smell of the lane, the laughter...

The man appeared—a shortish man who had been hiding in the mob. His small, quick eyes shone under his thick dense and long, bushy eyebrows giving him a canine look. With very slow steps he was moving towards Willie.

'Where's your darling?' he lifted Willie's chin with a jerk.

'Speak, where is she?'

Each time he asked the question, he dashed Willie's head against the wall and each time Willie's body swayed like a drunkard's... And they were laughing.

'Kick him there!'

Another man pointed to his crotch. Bang! Bang!... the sound of his head being pounded against the wall. Willie's shirt was spattered with sweat and blood. Bang, bang, incessant and endless...and weird laughter...

'Speak, where is she? Speak! Speak! Speak! You filthy...' Ha-ha-ha... Bang, bang, bang... The colourful roses flowing down the scarf.

I can't recall anything now. As a matter of fact, I do not even know if it was I who had cried out or whether it was somebody else's shriek which had shaken me so. (No, even today I can't believe that terrible shriek could have come out of my throat!) All I remember is my short rapid breath flitting desperately, like a bat, hitting the walls of my chest. With a wrench I freed my neck from the clutch that held me back.

Only two yards—and the darkness between us.

I leapt towards Willie. I wanted to tell him something. I wanted to touch him—it seemed to be of utmost importance then.

The intervening darkness... and those cold hands, and, that scream...

My head crashed against the invisible chin of the man who seized my arm as I fell forward. With his other hand, he clasped my face. My face rubbed against his shirt. 'I'll teach you to run... you fucking bastard!' I was blindly beating the air with my legs, like an epileptic. It's no use, I thought, he won't let go of me—and then it seemed impossible to breathe. But I was breathing all right, each breath breaking the spell of its predecessor, coming up one after the other, and clinging to me, coming up in succession, no breath wanting to be the last. And I was enveloped in an awful happiness as if this was the moment I had been longing for all my life and it had finally arrived and nothing in all the coming hours would bear the same meaning to me—no fear the same as the one I had known in the past. I forgot that I was all alone. I knew only that they were not going to leave me alone, that it was impossible for me to escape. For the first time, I realized in that night that it was not enough to be alone; not enough, for they were everywhere. And this I know. But what I did not know was that they were sure to catch me one day. It was no longer amorphous—the fear, I mean. It was concrete and well defined, as large as myself. We were both breathing, like two distinct hearts in the dark, and it seemed that I would go on kicking my legs up in the air just like that... oh, dear! How funny it is! How funny! Someone's laughing (Is it me?) laughter which has no sound... blows... abuses and then the same laughter again...

Where are they?

They had abandoned me in a filthy dark corner. I can't say how long I lay there, opening my eyes now and then to glimpse the sky of London shriveled behind a thin veil of mist. Then again my eyes closed and I felt as if I was traveling through one veil of mist into the next.

I don't know how long I remained in that state. When I came to, I heard footsteps coming up to me. Very slow. I wasn't fully awake. Maybe it was all a dream. For a long time I did not know that somebody was tugging at my shoulder.

'Are you much hurt?'

'No, not much.'

My eyes opened. Leaning over me I saw George's face. A weak smell of lager led me on to another patch of memory. A fragment of Mozart's 'Serenade'. Or, perhaps just a quiver, like a broken twig.

'You still here!' I exclaimed.

'I knew they had brought you here. I was watching,' he said.

'Where's Willie?'

'Let him go to hell... if he had not been there nothing would have happened, though...'

'What wouldn't have happened?'

Just then a car passed through the wide street. Our eyes were dazzled. For the first time my thoughts turned towards myself. My shirt collar was torn at the top; a clammy, heavy vapour emanating from the undershirt.

'Why did you come back?'

'I wanted to go inside... to you people, but...'

'It's all right, George!' I interrupted him. The taste in my mouth was sour like after a prolonged fever. I spat out into the heart of the yellow circle of light. There was a lamp-post near me. I spat scarlet as if I had been chewing a betel leaf. It was blood. It was strange! I spat once again—I couldn't suppress the urge to see the colour of my own blood again.

'Are you sure you aren't much hurt?' George said. There was a strange sense of guilt in his voice.

I kept quiet. And then I leapt to my feet. My head rested awhile against the wall... Bang... bang... bang... The sound still beat through my nerves.

Quietly we made for the station. I still had the shillings in my pocket. Unconsciously I was caressing them with my quivering fingers. The leaves of August were scattered all over the street, the London smog was dispersing.

'You don't trust me... You think...' abruptly George seized me by the shoulder.

'It's all right,' I shrugged his hand off. I wished he were not with me at that moment.

We descended the steps to the tube.

The platform was almost deserted. Only a few people sat on the benches, dozing. There was a couple behind the pole near us, close to the wall. The girl touched her own hair frequently. The young man stood in front of her whispering something in low tones. The girl burst out laughing now and again, casting a cautious glance about her.

We bought our tickets and sat down on a bench.

'You'll stay on in London?'

He kept quiet. He had his eyes set on the tunnel beyond the lights—a dark, damp tunnel, a darkness which was distinct from the darkness of the city above. It looked more like a blotch of dirty water.

'Goodness! You know where Willie is gone?'

'Willie? I didn't see him,' he said.

'But you just said you'd been standing outside.'

'I did not see anything.'

We fell silent again. But between us there was a wearying tension, as if something were returning to us again and again in spite of our driving it away.

'You think I'm lying,' he said.

I looked away.

'You may think what you like, I don't give a damn,' he said.

'Don't be silly,' I said.

'You don't trust me.' This time he looked up at me. 'You think I ran away...' His lips quivered. 'Damn it, I say damn it!'

'It's all right, George.'

'Oh, no, it's not all right,' he almost screamed.

'George, listen,' I placed my hand on his shoulder. He had his face pressed between both his hands and it quivered occasionally.

'I was afraid, terribly afraid.'

We were both trembling.

'Afraid...'.

I gazed in front of me. The underground station seemed to quiver, like a curtain about to go up. I was afraid of George, afraid of myself. It looked as though I would never be able to bring myself to set my eyes on him again. I wanted to talk to him, to tell him a great deal, but we were insulated from one another. Though we sat together, he was crying and there was nothing I could do. Perhaps nothing is more terrible than this... two persons, though together, abruptly realizing that neither of them can save the other...no remembrance not even one moment of the past hours lends a hand to alleviate the utter loneliness of the present, passing moment... With a start we saw the train bound for Warren Street arriving on the other platform. It was George's. People dozing on benches were waking up. The darkness in the New Acton tunnel had shrunk a little in the sharp headlight of the underground train. A few people came rushing down the stairs to the platform to catch their last train to Warren Street.

George stood up. He did not so much as glance at me and the next moment he was running towards the tube with the crowd. The automatic doors of the train opened for a moment and then closed almost at once, swallowing up the crowd.

The clattering of wheels gradually faded out, and calm returned. The darkness that had been pushed back by the headlight was back in its place.

You could see only the lights of New Acton, beyond the open roof of the platform, flickering quietly in the dark.

The young man behind the pole said, 'By the next train...' and kissed her. Her eyes closed. He did not even glance...

I felt as if I had not smoked for ages.

Gyan Prakash

Gyan Prakash (1932–2012), a prolific writer, known for his (eight collections of) short stories, with a distinct flavour of idiomatic language, ascerbic tongue, and sharp critical eye on his times. He also published a novel and a collection of poems; edited magazines like *Bahas* and a special number of *Tarang*; took part in protest movements launched by government employees.

Sincere Folks

Imaandar Log

I was glad, all too glad, that at long last my friend, caught in dire straits of privation, turbulence and predicaments had found an anchor. He had appeared in a number of academic exams and failed, and now when his heart was completely shattered and he was finding his life extremely savourless, desolate and worthless and had been contemplating suicide, success had come to his rescue. He had become an official of the Government of India, and thus, all of a sudden, it dawned upon him that life was but a pretty little garden of fragrant flowers, full of colours and gaiety and pleasure. This sudden transformation in him no doubt brought an ironical smile to my lips, but it vanished in a moment, and instead I was filled with contentment to see that he had finally arrived.

I could not keep my joy from my sweetheart, and in my zeal I even over-praised him. Driven by some unknown inspiration I had invented numerous qualities and abilities in my friend which in fact did not exist. My sweetheart was a teacher in an ordinary school and unmarried so far. She was a light dark woman of commonplace features and yet I don't know what it was that made me restless without her although I was married and had several children. In the initial phase of love, we had seriously discussed the probable consequences of our affair. I couldn't have forsaken my wife and children, nor sever my links with my beloved. Morally and socially I was bound to my family, while without my beloved my existence itself seemed to be meaningless. Without her I would be a living corpse, a conglomeration of flesh and hide. It was only in her companionship that my existence acquired a meaning and my personality a significance. With her, life was a resonance of sweet melody.

My own life was in fact a bitter tale of privations and humiliations for I was a clerk. And so my gratitude to my beloved knew no bounds at times who had accepted my courtship. I was a small individual whose sole utility—in the eyes of the society—lay in employing me in drudgery. It is true that I was often victim to an illusion that I was an able and intelligent man whose worth was not evaluated and thus was much wronged against. I consoled myself with the thought that they were all foolish and mean people and they only harmed themselves by refusing me my due, but it was only a private consolation. The fact was that I was a clerk, and I had to face rebukes from my boss, reminders of my creditors and the contemptuous eyes of my wife—which told me without uttering a word that I was a rotter, good-for-nothing.

The initial phase of our affair was over; both of us, that is she and myself, accepted our situation quite realistically. And I began to denigrate my wife and elevate my beloved: I would describe my wife as coarse, narrow-minded, petty and hoarse-throated, while my beloved looked cultured, well-mannered, generous and great. As for myself, I found that I was hopeless, a victim of society, religion and orthodoxy, surrounded by odd circumstances, condemned, miserable and neglected, sick of life, on the brink of ending my own life. I told my beloved all this and pointed out that, but for her, I would have put an end to my life. She was my only stay in a life where there was not one ray of hope. She was the only yarn in the fabric of a life gone to shreds, which kept it together.

My beloved was moved to the core as she heard me, her eyes agleam with tears. She would declare that I was great, sincere, selfless, sacrificing, talented and erudite. Her head leaning against my chest, she would ask me what'd happen to her after me? She, too, was living only for my sake. What else was there to bind her to life? She would continue—'you are a man, you stand to lose nothing, whereas I as a woman have to contend with thousand and one social restrictions'. But she could stand fearlessly against all those perils because of me she would declare, though she felt that she was sad, hapless and oppressed even more than I was, and so for the sake of one another, we eschewed suicide and lived on.

My beloved would tell me that I was the most handsome man in the world and that there was something divine about my personality which fascinated her most. She made fun of every other male we knew. This guy's teeth were too big, that guy's lips too fat, this one's head looked like a pumpkin, and so on and so forth. The crux of the matter was she would not approve of any masculine body other than mine. I was quite often taken in by such deceptive descriptions, but then I also realized that her loving eyes has only one image imprinted on them, that this was not an objective view but a subjective perception. In love everything is beautiful, grand and great, indeed!

Among the menfolk I used to be rather reticent. Silence was my armour. Different people had different views about my temperament. Some took me for a cool, sober man, while others thought that I was a simple, artless soul, and some others considered me dangerously quiet. To some I looked stupid and backward, while others thought that I was overly clever, pragmatic and opportunist. The only reason for these contradictory assessments was that I had withdrawn within myself like a tortoise and my mouth was never more active than a snail. I could be wise, but only after the event. Whenever I tried to say something funny, people would stare at me stonily as if I had said something incomprehensible. Embarrassed, I withdrew and by and by, I gave up even my occasional repartees and wisecracks. I preferred therefore to remain dumb. Among menfolk I got bored, and wondered at their petty, commonplace, foolish prattle. But sometimes their comments or phrases stuck in my mind and I used them profusely in front of my sweetheart. Her mere presence would make me an adroit conversationalist and I was able to spin a lot of yarn before her. Sometimes I was surprised at my own wittiness for many of the ideas I expressed before her had never before crossed my mind. And my jokes and witticisms made her roll over with laughter. She would declare with a thrill and affection that what she adored most in me was my art of conversation. It gave me a fathomless self-confidence and courage and strength and I began to think I could really talk original and extraordinarily in her company. She would be all ears, her eyes exuding admiration and awe, and those moments would convince me of my greatness which was being neglected by the petty beings of this world. In this vast world, only my sweetheart had the eye to perceive my worth. Naturally, I reciprocated. Who else but me could have penetrated her soul to find the unique greatness, the purity and the beauty which had remained similarly unrecognized! She had washed away all my prejudices against women. She had given me a new sight and I was immensely beholden to her for that!

She knew all about my friends, acquaintances and relations. She knew about the temperaments of my officers and colleagues. She was aware of my condition—financial, social and familial. Similarly, I knew about the politicking of her head-mistress and other teachers. She had no family of her own. Her parents were dead, leaving nothing behind for her. Getting married was a problem. But upon my entry into her life she had finally decided to refrain from wedlock. She was prepared to live as my second wife, but I would have forfeited my job in that event as I was a government servant. We could only curse our misfortune. Left to her income alone, she could not have fed my entire family if I lost the job. She helped me with money, too, on occasions, and I reciprocated the gesture though she rarely needed it, and haggling over accounts between us was naturally out of the question.

With such an intimacy between us, it was quite natural on my part to tell her about my friend-turned-official. His success seemed to me a sort of achievement of my own as well. And as it happens on such occasions, I was extravagant in narrating the success-story—I was speaking as if in a hysteria. Although I knew where I was lying, I enjoyed myself. I had added two hundred bucks to his actual emoluments. I told her he might one day go up to earn in four, even five figures. And his manner, his style of living, his way of talking...everything was unique! Indirectly and subtly I had of course given her enough hints of my own contribution in the making of my friend's personality and fortune.

I was certainly happy at my friend's rise, but not so much as I was making out. And on her part, it was most natural to show interest, appreciation and joy in something which apparently had given me so much happiness. She made up her mind to invite him to a celebration. My fondness of her grew by leaps and bounds at her generosity. It was much too late when I realized my idiocy, that I was actually cutting the ground from under my own feet.

The party was arranged. There were only three of us. She was in her best make-up. I had known her most intimately, but never before had I imagined that she could be that beautiful with ornaments and make-up. She was fluttering like a butterfly. Her enthusiasm knew no limits. She was entirely a new being. I was stunned. My eyes grew ever-thirsty and at the same time I felt a pain. Was it sort of a foreboding?

My friend wore an extremely sober countenance, almost with an aura of a celebrity about himself. He looked important. I was witnessing a new, unknown soul in him. Something new, but not quite amiable; a sense of horror and distance. What was it?

I was in an odd position between these two angles. Unwittingly I was gripped with a sense of inferiority and my ego took up an impenetrable armour of reticence. Separately in the company of each of them I was given to eloquence. But that day in those moments I lost my tongue. A flood of anger arose in me, an impotent violence reared its head. I withdrew within myself, detached from the environs.

Soon, they were laughing without restraint. They questioned me from time to time about my sudden silence. I forged a smile in reply. I listened to them with anguish, intermittently giving out a loud guffaw for no apparent reason, which in fact startled them. I had been dear and near to both of them. I found that they had been talking mostly about me, exchanging anecdotes and enjoying themselves. As they grew anxious over my nonchalance, I told them I was not well. They readily accepted my alibi and plunged back into their mutual world. My presence had become quite ridiculous and miserable. I wished to flee from there, but it would have appeared too childish and crude. I sat on.

It was only to keep up appearance that I ate. Nothing was palatable, though she had never before cooked such varieties and delicacies. I had ate there many a time. Sometimes by chance, at other times when I had a quarrel with my wife. She cooked well with interest and affection. But her fare usually was simple. It gave you a subtle pleasure. But today! As if it were a party for the governor-general. And how solicitously she was offering him food, as if he were her fiancé!

I found myself unable to face them. Was I guilty of anything to them? Was I humiliated? If not, then how did I land in such a condition?

Finally the time for farewell arrived. They exchanged promises for their probable meeting again. I returned home, sad, crestfallen, feigning a severe headache. Life had drained out of me and I was burning with helpless rage. My throat had dried and my eyes hurt. By instinct and sheer habit I had reached home and given a knock on the door.

My wife opened the door. She complained of my late arrival, with her sleepy, tired eyes and drowsy voice and then proceeded to curse her own fate. Well, enough is enough! Raging from inside I suddenly burst up and lashed out against her cheeks. In my blindness and madness I had beaten up my poor innocent wife. No, it was not my wife that I had hit—the body belonged to my wife but my aim was someone else. But she was the one who suffered. And I suffered. As if I were intoxicated. I was not I, but a beast, a carnivore, a sadist. No, I was a coward, a dastard. But who can say if those two were not cowards and dastards as well, that they were not hiding something from me!

In the dead of night I was listening to the suppressed, pitiful, helpless sobbing of my wife. She was suffering injustice and oppression.

Full of repentance, I threw my head into her lap and cried bitterly. Was I sorry for beating her, or was it some other pain?

My wife stopped crying as soon as she saw me weep. She began to pat and console me. I wept till the tears lay heavy on my chest, frozen into stones.

My hunch was not baseless. I went to my sweetheart's but a lock on the door welcomed me. I went to my friend's but I found him missing. Alone and distressed and hurt I wandered in the streets. I avoided the recognizing eyes in the streets.

But one day I caught them together. My heart began to sink. My head reeled ferociously. I couldn't keep myself on my feet and returned straight to my own home.

I wanted to hate them, but I had lost my capacity to feel anything. I had reached the stage where I could not tell one feeling from the other. An attitude of total negation—where there was only non-sensitivity to hatred or love, duty or existence. I wanted to cry, but couldn't. I wanted to kill them, but my hands seemed lifeless. I wanted to give them back for their deception and perfidy, but my tongue refused to stir. A kind of meaninglessness had over-powered me.

Both life and nature seemed to be utterly devoid of a moral fabric. As if some unknown libertarian and demonic force were guiding and governing everything. Nothing seemed to possess any logical unity. Was this great creation doomed, I wondered.

It took me a long time to recover. And then I tried to ascertain the flow of my thoughts and action. Those from whom I had derived so much happiness, whose companionship had given the meaning and direction to my life, in whom I had reposed confidence and who had been the source of my strength and inspiration—they had no hitch, not even a moment, in cheating and betraying me. I looked inside myself. How sincere I had been toward my sweetheart? I loved her, no doubt, but I could not marry her. She loved me and wanted to marry me. She required a marriage for a respectable place in the society. She had turned to my friend for this only. But already his marriage had been settled with another girl. My friend had betrayed both me and my beloved. Was it to see this day that I had dissuaded him from suicide! Does a person, dissuaded from suicide, plunge himself subsequently into committing homicides!

My lover had betrayed me, but why? I had kept her under false illusions, but why? My friend had betrayed us both, but how could he succeed in betraying both of us?

I had been living a life both with my wife and my beloved. With this double falsehood, I was sincere and insincere at the same time, I reasoned.

Perhaps, all three of us had been both sincere and insincere at the same time.

Mahendra Bhalla

Mahendra Bhalla (1933–2015), writer of short stories, novels, plays and poetry, is a renowned personality in the world of Hindi literature. His memorable plays include *Dimaag-e-hasti, Dil Ki Basti Hai Kahan, Hai Kahan*. His stories, and a trilogy of novels on the Indian immigrants in England is particularly reavealing. Hindi Akademi Award among several other honours were conferred on him.

Doggery

Kuttegiri

About two things I had never shown any curiosity to him. One, when did he find the time for his own work? He himself had volunteered: 'I import dry fruits from Pakistan. That keeps me going. As for the rest, well, I'm free to indulge in my doggery.'

'Doggery?'

'You don't know? Never mind. You will know it by and by.'

From his complacent smile it seemed he was rather fond of this thing he had just mentioned. But when, at what hour, could he be earning for his dough? For I see him all the time hanging about the coffee house. He was sure to materialize, as if from nowhere, even if you missed to spot him at first glance. Look there he comes!

'Hello, Sahni! Free?'

'For you I'm always free—be it day or night, storm or avalanche. Always at your service, as they say!'

This was his usual gambit and both of us laughed. Some men around us were looking in our direction. It was the same group he was normally seen with.

'Your pals are watching you,' I said.

'They're all friends here. Let them be.' Yet he turned his face towards them to exchange pleasantries.

'I see them every day, but you are a rare bird. And, of course, it's always something special when one meets with you.'

'You are getting adept at pulling other people's legs, Sahni!'

'Now, don't Bharadwaj!' He seemed to wince at my simple remark, as if I had rebuked him for his favourite—doggery.

'But, Sahni, I'm here practically every day!' This seemed to assuage him a bit.

'That's good—really good. You'll also soon fall in line.'

It was alarming. He had already somehow smelled that I too was going to join the ranks of all those who hang about Connaught Place for want of anything better to do? I began to size him up in my mind. He looked married all right, though I had never seen him with his wife. I generally judge men when they are with their wives, and this was the other thing about which I had refrained from asking him so far. Why did he never bring his wife and children along even for an outing to Connaught Place?

'What will you have?' I asked.

'The same good old hot coffee!' He responded as usual. And having uttered this, as always, he was again all ears, ready to lap up anything escaping my tongue. This particular gesture of his never failed him. My ego did get a boost and I felt somewhat relieved of my acute loneliness. My days, after all, were given to loitering and nothing else!

I ordered some *vada*s and coffee. The *vada*s had already gone cold. I only took a few bites and began to sip my coffee.

'You haven't finished your *vadas*,' said Sahni.

'No. They are cold and tasteless.'

'Not so bad, eh!' He said as he picked up the remains from my plate.

'Let us get some more if you like them,' I offered. 'Why should you pick up the left-overs!'

'Did you say left-overs?' Sahni murmured.

We were both used to eating from one another's plate, yet it occurred to me that he somehow lacked in self-respect. The way he gobbled up those crumbs, dipping them into the ketch-up in my plate.

But he was enjoying his coffee.

This was the hour when the coffee house begins to swarm with people. Quite a few were sitting vacantly on the low-lying wall that made for a fence. Some were in the lawns beyond the wall. A cup of coffee and being a part of the vibrant multitude around filled us with an animal satisfaction. We felt less lonely.

Suddenly there appeared an army of parakeets, shrieking and screeching, swooping down over the area. All eyes turned towards the sky. Trees stood swamped by the swarms of birds and their uproar, their green suffused with a brilliant fragrance of a water-melon-like sun in the clear, rain-time evening.

'We human beings have just one Coffee House, but these parakeets—they have by the thousands, I bet! They also debate and discuss among themselves.' Sahni was again his usual absurd self.

'Doggery?' I needled him.

'They are all real doggers... and not just them. All birds.' He insisted.

'Then why not call it parakeetery?'

'Do, if you wish. However, doggery is the thing. Dogs are dogs even if they live in a city.'

He was staring at the sky. Thousands of birds took off from their perches and started soaring over us in higher and higher circles. At a certain point in their spiral flight, the setting sun lit up their under-bellies in an uncanny luminosity.

'See?' Sahni struck in.

'Saw.'

Both of us laughed.

'Too many people at one place.'

'Where else would they go? They all come rushing in. They sit and gossip. What else would they do?'

I did not understand him. Nor did I try to. It was suddenly twilight, and equally abruptly it occurred to me that being with Sahni was just not enough. I wanted to be home, at once. And yet I was scared of it. I would be lying all by myself in my room—a stupidity I committed all too often.

'Do you care for a whisky, Sahni?'

'I don't mind.'

I need not have asked him. Instead, I should have told him, 'Come Sahni, let's have some whisky!' And he would have tagged along.

Entering a wine shop, for a moment I thought of giving it up. Just this morning I had realized that I would have to manage for at least another fortnight with the small amount of money left in my pocket. It was no longer easy to raise a loan. Even so, I took out my wallet with a suicidal flourish, bought half a bottle, and made for the door.

Outside, it was a changed world. We had entered the shop when it was still dusky. But now full darkness had descended. Lights in the shops and streets were on. Shadows worked mystery in the open empty spaces. Something strange seemed to hover about the faces of people. A hint of hope seemed to ignite in that electric light, which would have been impossible to conjure up in the daytime.

'Saw?' spoke up Sahni. Even he was thrilled.

I didn't respond. Instead, my eyes kept wandering.

'See, over there!'

I drew his attention to a girl. A whore... I was smiling half hoping that Sahni would also join in, just as two cohorts do when they spot a whore.

It made me uneasy when he didn't. Again I threw a glance at the girl. The same fatty one, often seen in these corridors.

'Saw?' I mimicked, to please Sahni. But he didn't utter a word. Instead, he began to walk faster, the bottle under his arm. The girl also looked in our direction. I had a hunch that they somehow knew each other. My curiosity had the better of me.

'I know her,' I said.

'How?'

'She used to live in the same street where I did. They are three sisters, aren't they? They all have whiskers! The other two are employed. This one is in the profession. She, too, shaves. Doesn't she?'

He was standing in the middle of the crowd listening to me. His face showed interest, tension and nervousness.

'Who knows!' He feigned nonchalance and moved on.

I looked back as we were turning a corner.

'Still there?' Sahni did not look at me, yet he had guessed that I had turned to look back at the girl.

'Yes, still there.'

'What's her name?' he asked me.

'I don't know, but surely you must be knowing?'

'Yes...no...how should I know?' But he could not see me in the eye and he knew I was smiling.

We began to drink. Sitting on the terrace in front of Gupta's office. Gupta's man had brought us soda, etc., and he was sitting in a corner, gazing down on the street below. In between, he would get up and go into the room, perhaps to answer the phone.

Practically, only two of us were there. Gupta had not come. His chair lay vacant before us. Sometimes both of us simultaneously glanced at the chair. It was made from cane, and its inky shadows made a pattern on the window panes.

'This Gupta...he works a lot.'

'Yes, he makes a lot of money.'

'You, too, make a lot of it, and that without working as hard...!'

'Oh, it's a different matter. I've my own way of doing it.'

'Let me also know, yaar! I wish I could also strike it rich for no effort at all. And if slog you must, it should be minimal. Once you are in money, life becomes so easy! Yes?'

'You're wrong,' he spoke with so much vehemence in his voice that I felt I was wrong indeed. I also loathed myself for this sort of dreaming which never left me, though I was a grown-up man now.

'One should not work too hard,' he said, evading my original question.

'Why?'

'Work creates delusions. Work is an opiate.'

'How?' I was baffled.

He kept quiet. Instead, he lifted his glass and began to look into the whisky.

We were mildly drunk.

The noises of Connaught Place seemed to waft up from somewhere deep below. Perhaps from an abyss. Both of us soared in the air. Mutually entwined.

'Work! What does one work for?' he asked. And then replied himself, 'You work so that you can earn money and kill time.

Though one would never like to work to kill time—if one had the money. What do you say?'

I couldn't think of any answer. Silently, I watched him.

'And, then, work is a delusion. Here we are—sitting, thinking, talking... There is a sky above us, but we can't see it because there is a lamp burning over our heads. There are shafts of light coming from down below, and an uproar from Connaught Place... as if from an abyss. We are a little drunk.'

So, he also felt that the noises from Connaught Place reminded him of an abyss! Strange! I looked at him intently. There was a spot of light sitting on his bald pate, and in the deep pits under his eyebrows, two needle-sharp, light-red bulbs had lit up.

It seemed to me that instead of Sahni, his ghost was with me. It almost frightened me. I turned my eyes towards the peon who was still sitting in the corner, but so still and motionless that he didn't seem real. I saw from where I sat, the shadow of the chair but not the chair. As if to reassure myself, I turned again towards 'Sahni'. He was laughing. I shuddered.

'Look here! The real thing to do is to do nothing. There is nothing out there anywhere.' He raised his hands skywards in a half circle. There was nothing there, indeed. Yet, I looked up in vain.

Sahni began to hum and the 'maya' was shattered. It seemed as if I had cottonwool balls thrust into my ears, and now they had dropped out.

I began to laugh as I looked at him.

'Why, Sahni, you are a philosopher to boot!'

'I told you the truth, pure and unadulterated.'

'Do you call it doggery?'

'Partly. Let us say, this is where it begins.'

In order to make the atmosphere look human again, I called out to the peon to get us some ice. As soon as he stirred, the eeriness vanished.

We filled up our glasses.

'To your doggery!' I intoned, raising my glass.

'Damn! You are making fun of it.'

He was tense. I was laughing. Abruptly I stopped.

'Work etcetera are nothing but excuses to escape. One must always be in the forefront—to bear the brunt.' His tone carried a challenge.

'But dogs generally run away.'

'All right, but from whom? May be from the human beings, or from other dogs, or something else. But they never try to escape that!'

'That—what?'

'From that!...that...rather they'd wander, loaf around and sleep in that itself.'

I did not argue with him. His unshapely face looked miserable. More so, if you gave it a long stare. Just then I discovered a great resemblance between him and a dog. His ears were long and his double-barrel nose lay close to his thick, wet lips.

'Putchh! Putchh...!' I found myself addressing him, involuntarily the way one does a dog. But suddenly I thought that may be my face also resembles a dog's? I tried in vain to recall the image of my own face. I looked about for a mirror desperately. I wanted to run to the bathroom to have a look at my face.

But just then I realized that I was probably losing my balance. I made an effort. I overcame this sudden urge and smiled at Sahni. 'Tell me, Sahni! I've never seen you with your family...

I mean, are you married?' The doubt about his being married at all grew as I put the question. That was why I had changed my question.

'Family? Whose?'

'Yours! Who else's?'

'I and a family! Brother, it's not in my line.'

'Why?'

'Excuse me, Bharadwaj, but is marriage at all a human affair?'

'Dogs and cats do not marry, I'm sure.'

He suppressed his laughter and said, 'I don't think it's the right thing.'

'But without this, how... I mean how...'

'I know,' he said, 'there are various ways.'

'Tell me one.'

He fell silent. I prodded him, 'One of the ways surely was the one we met with in the corridor.'

'Okay, that's one.'

'I think that one is the only effective way.'

'There are other ways.'

'For example?'

He was silent.

'Tell me,' I pressed him.

He regarded me for a while with vacant eyes, then began to pour the last peg of whisky, his head bowed. After a sip, he smiled.

'Now, out with it, yaar!' I was insistent.

He kept smiling, then gulped another draught of whisky. Perhaps he was bluffing, I thought. He just wanted to impress me. I noticed one of his feet touched the empty chair and he was shaking it rather merrily. Merrily—not out of uneasiness, which should have been the case for being unable to respond. He was obviously enjoying himself.

Suddenly it occurred to me that he was making a fool of me, and that he had been doing this all along. Always cheating me—drinking coffee and whisky out of me, all under the guise of a feigned submission. If that was part of his doggery, he is certainly a successful dogger.

With this shocking realization, my temper rose. I struggled within myself to contain the anger, but gradually I had reached a point where my desire to take revenge—to hurt him—had already crystallized.

'Sahni, let me tell you something. You know, I've a friend who decided to marry some two or three years back. Looking for a suitable girl, he found one. She was educated, modern. When he was talking to her in her house—her parents and other relatives were also there—she abruptly got up and went inside the house. My friend distracted himself with coffee, tea, etc., for a while, happy in the thought that his search for a girl was over. He had found one who was beautiful and good. But suddenly he heard a voice coming from behind the curtain near him. He claims it was the same girl speaking, and that she was alone behind the curtain. She was talking to herself only to let him overhear... She had said...who'd marry this pig-faced...'

I paused to look at Sahni.

'Although I thought my friend was quite good-looking, he was so shaken at that incident that he has refused to marry ever since...'

'You are right,' said Sahni, 'I'm ugly.'

There was a mild tremor in his voice and I felt a sense of regret. However, thinking it would be foolish to apologize now, I lied. 'You're mistaken. You are not like that at all—'

'As if I wouldn't know, eh!' he said and became quiet.

He looked pulled down, absorbing the hurt I had inflicted on him. But he did not show any resentment. In a flash, he had revealed all of himself to me. He belonged to that tribe of people who are rarely, if ever, hurt, try as you may to torment them. They even seem to enjoy it in a certain way, and would use it to maintain friendship deep down for their own selfish ends.

Yet, I was embarrassed.

'Beauty and ugliness are rather subjective notions,' I clutched at the straw of a cliché, in order to break the silence.

'I better tell you,' Sahni volunteered, drawing himself a bit forward. 'The girl we saw outside the wine shop, who has taken to prostitution now, does come from my own area. I knew her family and she knew mine. You have seen her face. She looks four times uglier in the daylight. At that time I did not admit it to myself but that was the reason I took interest in her. I had thought it would click with her in no time.

'Somehow it tarried on. I even visited her home once or twice. But our conversations remained formal. By that time she had already left off her studies. I dared not say anything in the presence of her people, and she never seemed to go out of her home.

'One day, as I was roaming about in the university, I saw her coming from the opposite direction. I was surprised to see her there. I could never have imagined that she could ever come to the university area! I thought it had a special meaning.

'I started walking with her. In that evening hour she didn't look ugly; rather she seemed a bit pretty. I noticed that her gait was attractive and supple. She had a well-built figure, which gave rise to a hope in me—perhaps, we could, after all, bear life together. But this hope put a lump in my throat. And I was unable to utter a word.

'Then she stopped walking and said to me, "Okay, then, come home some time?"

"I will!"

'As she turned to walk away from me, I cursed my own spinelessness—I was nervous in front of a girl like her! I pulled myself together and called out to her and told her what I wanted to.

'She broke into a hearty laughter.

"You're uglier than me," she told me, and laughed again. In fact she went on laughing in such an irrepressible manner that after the initial hesitation even I joined her in her candid laughter. For a few moments we were both laughing heartily and with a strange openness, perhaps like two sisters.

'Then both of us fell silent. She turned round and walked away from me without a word.

'My people continued to pester me for marriage, but I always refused. Ultimately they also gave up.'

'Well!' That was all I could say.

'For, how long can anybody keep trying to persuade you? And, anyway, there was no need. Even without a marriage you can have everything.'

'How?'

'Eh!'

He had been truthful so far, but now he was prevaricating.

I didn't like it. I fixed my eyes on him for a while, even though I knew my stare meant little to him.

'Do you know how old I am?' He surprised me with his query. Whisky had made him crimson and younger.

'Around thirty-three, I guess!'

'You're right. Thirty-four'. He looked crestfallen, perhaps because I was able to make an accurate guess.

'One gets wise at this age.'

'I don't know', I said stiffly.

Perhaps my tone was too harsh, for he looked at me with a start, and then with a bowed head he gripped his glass. I was about to fall into a sense of regret again, when I noticed him raising his glass to drain it to the last drop. He put down the glass and smacked his lips.

A realization suddenly stabbed me. This guy was merely interested in passing an evening, caring a hoot for truth or falsehood.

'I've been cheated', I told myself and this thought incensed me. Quite beside myself. I got up and flung a string of words at him: 'Whisky is finished. Let us get going now!'

Both of us climbed down the stairs and began to walk in the Connaught Place corridors. I was a little ahead of him while he was sort of dragging himself behind me.

'Listen, Bharadwaj', he tried to strike a conversation. I did not respond. The corridors were empty and dark. We saw a few people here and there, more like shadows.

In a few strides he caught up with me and again tried to talk. I only grimaced. I wonder if he could notice it in the darkness. However, his attempt was lost and he began to walk quietly, without trying to talk again.

Now that I had completely subdued him, I began to melt. I stopped in front of a dhaba where we sometimes ate. He, too, stopped.

'I shall be taking leave of you now', he said.

'Won't you eat something?'

'No'.

'Why?'

'Well, I don't feel like it.'

'Have a little bit.'

'No.' He was adamant.

'Come on, what's the matter, Sahni?' I said with a sudden affection.

'Yaar, you don't like me'.

I had never thought he could be so childlike at heart. Suppressing an urge to cry, I said, 'Come on, Sahni, you're mistaken', and put my arm around his shoulders.

'No, No—' He tried to free himself. But I held on to him and holding him thus, I dragged him into the dhaba. We took a table and sat down facing each other. But for a long while we could not look into each other's eyes. Talking seemed impossible. We were at our wit's end.

We began to eat.

'Meat is good.'

'Yes!'

Silence. A motley smell arose from the tandoor—of chapatti, vegetables, smoke and of dirty furniture, all mixed together.

'Have some more chapatti!'

'No.'

'Take one at least.'

'No. That'll do.'

After eating, we came out of the dhaba.

'Where will you go?' I asked him.

'Coffee House. Come along!'

'No, I'll go home.'

'All right, then, tomorrow?'

'I'm not sure,' I said.

He turned and walked away towards the Coffee House. I watched him. He was about to disappear from sight behind the auto-rickshaw stand when suddenly I had a queer feeling. It won't make any difference anywhere even if he were to die tomorrow. I instinctively decided not to see him ever again.

After an interview for a job the next day, I ambled along the corridors of Connaught Place, and then went into the American Library, and for sometime, flipped through a glossy picture magazine. Coming back to Connaught Place again, I took a round of the circle.

Suddenly my eyes fell on two girls—very beautiful and very rich. It was an extreme torment—watching them. I felt my life was worthless—just like Sahni's.

And then, a craving welled up from within me for a quiet cup of coffee and a cigarette. I began to walk in the direction of the Coffee House.

Ram Narayan Shukla

Ram Narayan Shukla (1936–68) was a proficient writer whose works have immensely contributed to the development of the post-independence Hindi literature. His works are evident of the abundance of experimentation and novelty in the Hindi short story in the 1960s after the waves of the new story.

Brother of Mahendra

Mahendra Ka Bhai

I haven't come across a person like him again in my life! His face was shadowed by a peculiar misery. He had often dirty and sometimes even torn clothes on him. He sat quietly on the last bench, and just laughed when the boys pulled his leg. As soon as the class was over, he went out to stand by himself either in the empty space opposite the classroom, or in the verandah, as it took about ten to fifteen minutes to start the next class. He just stood there, watching the boys below.

I had enrolled myself in the third year in an evening college. The classes were held from six to nine o'clock. Four periods a day. Most of the students were employed and so they did not take their studies too seriously. They talked a lot among themselves when the teacher was not there. At times, when he did not feel like going out, he would sit in silence, listening to their conversation. He spoke little. From time to time, he would ask the boys about their jobs, and at such moments his eyes shone with a gleam. As if he were about to sink into an abyss.

That day I was late in reaching the college. The teacher was writing something on the black board. Quietly I entered and sat down in the last row. Later I noticed that I was sitting beside him.

He was listening quietly to the lecturer. Two or three times I glanced at him. It seemed as if he wanted to tell me something. It was a class of economics. I am quite interested in the subject. But I don't know why, perhaps due to his proximity, I was not able to follow the lecture properly.

He moved up closer to me as soon as the teacher left the room. I was just getting up when he asked me, rather nervously, 'Are you working somewhere?'

'No, I'm not. My father has a shop. Sometimes I have to attend to it.' I didn't want to tell him all this and yet I had blurted out everything.

He paused for a while after I had finished. Then he said, thoughtfully, 'You haven't been able to get a job so far?'

I was surprised at the question. 'Where is the question of getting one, I haven't even tried for it,' I said after a pause.

His face showed relief at this answer.

Both of us remained sitting in the same position for some time. The benches in the front row were empty and once the thought of going and sitting there crossed my mind. But somehow I didn't feel like getting up.

Just then he himself said, 'My name is Gajendra.'

I felt like laughing. He was very frail and his name (the king of elephants) seemed ridiculous compared to his physique.

At that point the teacher came in.

Two or three days after that, I was glancing at the notice board outside the office when he came up and stood behind me.

I did not pay any attention to him. There was a rush in the office. Students had queued up to deposit their fees. The college office often reminds one of a bank in a busy commercial area.

'Listen', he said hesitantly.

I gave him a careful look. He seemed to be in trouble. He was holding a large piece of paper and his hands were trembling.

'Yes?'

He said nothing. It seemed that he didn't want to talk, standing at that place.

Without saying anything, he started down the stairs. At first I could not figure it out, then I too followed him.

Downstairs in a solitary corner he asked me with some hesitation, 'Do you know any MLA or MP, or a gazetted officer?'

'Why?' It just escaped my lips.

He laid the form in my hands. It was a form for freeship. It had been filled up. It required recommendation from two eminent persons. There was a blank space for one signature.

'You see. I have obtained one with great difficulty. If you could get me the other one, I would submit it in the office,' he told me as I looked at the blank space.

I don't particularly know anybody in such circles. Perhaps I would myself find it difficult if ever a need arose. Yet there was something in the way he spoke and I had to take it seriously.

'I'll try,' I handed him back his form. 'It will surely be done in a day or two.'

I looked at the watch. It was no use going to the class now. Twenty-five minutes of the first period were over. The second would start after twenty minutes. Let us have tea in the canteen, I thought.

I told him my idea about tea in the canteen. He accompanied me without a word.

We were sipping our tea. I don't know why, it was hot, though it was not summer. Just then I felt that he wanted to say something. Something, about which he felt embarrassed.

'Why are you so quiet? Say something,' I said, trying to remove his hesitation.

'Have you really never searched for a job?' His face went almost pale as he said this.

It seemed an odd question. I did not reply.

'You see, you have taken it ill,' he tried to smile as he continued, 'it just escaped my lips. The trouble is I don't know how to put things properly.'

'No, it is all right. I didn't mind at all. You haven't said anything that one could feel bad about. Indeed I have never looked for a job.'

The bell rang before he could say anything further. Both of us got up and walked up to the classroom in silence.

The other day as we were having a chat, suddenly he broke in, 'Why do you talk in Bengali with me? It is no use at all.'

I was surprised. Usually I talk in Bengali with all Bengali boys. And they feel happy when they hear others talk in Bengali. I found it odd that Gajendra should feel the contrary. Even so, I did not say anything.

'You see,' he resumed after some time, 'it is no use to any one of us talking in Bengali. Why not talk in English instead? I've heard that those who speak English well, find it easier to get employed.'

I didn't say anything. I just glanced on at his ever-moist eye-lids.

After a pause he said, 'You know both Hindi and Bengali. Probably they prefer to employ such people. Teach me Hindi!'

'It isn't a difficult thing. If you want, you can learn Hindi very soon.'

We had been talking in a commonplace restaurant near the college. The third period was economics. The teacher did not turn up. What sort of a man is he! Half his classes go waste like this. Doesn't turn up.

Suddenly there was a noise, many people speaking all at the same time. Out on the street we found a sizeable crowd. A pickpocket had been nabbed red-handed.

From a distance I could see, his lips were bleeding, his face was lashed from a severe beating. I wanted to close my eyes, I feel giddy at the sight of blood. I looked back at Gajendra behind me. He was talking to some Bengali gentleman.

'Why do they hit so badly?' suddenly, unwittingly, I commented.

'I was saying the same thing to him', the Bengali gentleman said in a very soft tone. 'It shouldn't be done.'

I didn't say anything, though he wanted to continue the conversation. Gajendra joined me as he saw me withdraw from there.

'He is our age,' said Gajendra, abruptly.

'Hmm...' I muttered, just for the sake of it.

'Perhaps he failed to get a job.'

I did not comment.

Gajendra had gradually become a butt of ridicule for the entire class. They had started making fun of me, too, since they had noticed me moving with him. I didn't care.

When you looked at Gajendra's face, often it seemed as if he were preparing himself for a battle with some unknown force. Sometimes his face showed fear as though someone were about to strike him with a sword-like weapon. He lived in a horror, I did not know why.

One day when we were sitting in a park, he said in a very hushed voice, 'Is it very difficult to get a job?'

'It can be got. After all, so many people succeed in the search,' said I.

'I've never tried for it. I am frightened even to think of it. If I tried and didn't get one, then? I think I will plunge into the search after I pass my bachelors.'

The topic was not to my liking, so I kept quiet.

'I might have told you I had a second division in Inter.' Noticing that I was quiet, he said, 'After that many people advised me to try for a job, but I didn't. I kept wondering what would happen if I should fail in spite of my efforts. That is why I have decided to look for it only after my bachelors. I might even get it then.'

'So many people are able to get employment, why wouldn't you?' I said persuasively.

He was not bad at studies. He picked up things very quickly. He had got fairly good marks in the third year. He even scored the highest marks in the class in one or two subjects. I had told him when I saw his mark sheet, 'You have got good marks indeed.'

'What's the use! These are not even put on record. It would have been enough just to pass! Job...'

'Oh, leave it,' I changed the topic. 'But still, you should be happy.'

He did not say anything. He folded the mark sheet and put it in his pocket.

It was our first day as fourth years. The boys were cheerful. Usually no one is failed in the third year. But this time they had failed quite a few. The successful boys were, therefore, naturally happy.

There was a lot of commotion when I entered the class. Gajendra was talking to a boy beside him on the last bench. He looked less dejected than usual.

I started talking with the boys in the front row. They were all talking about the interception of so many boys in the third year for the first time.

The teacher did not turn up in the first period. We chatted throughout. After some twenty minutes I joined Gajendra on his bench. He managed to smile as he saw me. The smile filled his face and he seemed quite attractive.

We had a long discussion about the films on in the city. I had promised him a film show on passing the examination. We were trying to select a film.

Presently he said, musingly, 'You never wear a tie!'

It seemed a strange question. Like all his other questions. 'Never, so far,' I replied in spite of myself.

'I too don't wear it. I feel I must. Perhaps it impresses them in interviews for job, etc.'

'It isn't important', I said with a slight smile. 'It makes no difference whether you wear a tie or not.'

Then he fell silent. Looking at his face I knew he was still pondering over the same thing.

Days passed by. Throughout the day I would sit in the shop, and in the evening, go to the college. At times it all appeared absurd. Studying in an evening college is no study in the real sense. Even the three hours were not utilized every day. One day there would be only one period, the next day two. It became difficult to pass time when there was no class. Some boys had devised a regular programme for the free periods. They would either read in silence in an empty classroom, or play carom, chess, or table tennis. I didn't do all this. I liked to play chess, but usually one had to quit at an unfinished game or waste another period along with the free period to finish it.

One such day, when there was a free period, I went into the common room. I found Gajendra there, playing chess with another boy. Gajendra was in a strong position. He was likely to win. But the next period was to start barely within seven minutes. The game would not conclude within that time.

When the bell rang, I asked him to leave the game and come to the class. But he refused. I was rather surprised. It was the first time he hadn't attended a class while he was present there.

I left him playing.

In the third period he entered the class. His face looked terribly sad. I found it surprising. Why this quick change in his countenance!

He came over and sat down quietly beside me.

'What is the matter? Why are you so sad?'

'I lost the game. You had seen that I was winning'.

'So what! What is there to be so sad about it? Once I lost three games in succession'.

'No, the thing is...' he said hesitantly, 'I was thinking I would get a job if I win, but if...'

'Nonsense! I am afraid you will go mad like this. Why do you brood so much over such matters?'

He looked at my face quite idiotically.

Recently his face always reminded me of soldiers at war seeing the bombs falling on them from the sky. It seemed as if he were unable to devise any self-defence against the attack.

He had grown weaker. Sometimes he looked drowsy and wanting to go to sleep.

One day I asked him by the way, 'Why have you joined BCom? Perhaps BA honours would have been better.'

'I had consulted some people', he said, looking down at the floor. 'BCom has better prospects for employment than BA. That's why I took this course.'

I did not comment. Then he himself added, 'Sometimes I shudder at the thought of the coming days. I don't know anyone who could help me get a job. They say the ads. for "wants" in papers are worthless.'

I kept listening. I did not feel like saying a word, I don't know why.

It was Sunday. I was watching the cool waves of the Ganga at the Outram Ghat. There I caught sight of Gajendra sitting at some distance from me. He was looking at the innumerable lights glittering on the other bank.

His face seemed desolate in the faint glow of the lights. He closed his eyes off and on. For a long time I didn't feel like going over to him. He had not noticed me. But ultimately I got up and sat down beside him. He was startled to see me.

'I usually come here, just like that. I am fond of looking at these small boats sailing beside the ships'.

I did not say anything. We sat on for long. I was feeling uneasy sitting like this, without a word.

Suddenly Gajendra's lips quivered. 'My face usually looks sad, doesn't it?' He asked with his eyes on me.

I did not reply and he continued, 'Yesterday I was reading that they don't like to employ sad and sorrowful faces. I try to be cheerful, but...'

'You often talk very strangely', I told him for the first time, although on earlier occasions, I had been at the verge of saying it. 'I can't decide what one could say in reply'.

He was silent as he heard me out and he fell to brooding again.

The other day he had come to my home, for the first time. We had talked for long. All kinds of matter.

I went down to see him off to the gate. We talked for about five minutes on the footpath also. Then he walked away.

I was going up towards my room after his departure, when I met Amar babu on the steps. He lives on the floor above ours. He is doing research at the University. We talk frequently with one another.

'How did you come to know this boy?' He asked me as soon as he saw me.

'He studies with me. Why? Do you know him?' I asked in surprise.

'Yes', he said very slowly, 'he is the brother of Mahendra. Mahendra was my classmate in the college. Some two or three years ago he committed suicide, weary of being unemployed'.

Suddenly I recalled a lot of things Gajendra had been saying.

The House

Makaan

Only a while ago the attorney was talking to my elder uncle. Now nobody is speaking. All of us are listening to our own breathing. I throw a quick glance at the face of the buyer's attorney. There is nothing. Perhaps he is not thinking anything, or perhaps he is wishing that all this should end as quickly as possible so that he is relieved.

He has a small leather bag with him which contains currency notes worth eighty thousand rupees. It will all be ours and the large house about one and a half miles from here will accrue to his client.

They say the buyer has no kith or kin, except for a pregnant widow who is his daughter-in-law. He is buying the house for the baby in womb. The baby will be born in an all-owned house, a large one at that.

And we are selling away the house. Why? I do not know. I know many a thing, but nothing is clear.

I had never seen my family people in such numbers at one place, sitting together. There are eleven shares in all, and nine of them are present. Those absent are my two brothers. Both minors. Father will sign in their behalf. He is their guardian, de jure as well as de facto.

I, too, would have been absent, had they sold it a year ago. I attained majority only six months ago. I am the youngest among those present.

I look at my elder uncle. He is the eldest. I have never seen him laugh. Perhaps he just can't. He has never done a thing which could earn him a laughter. His eyes are fixed on my face. I wonder why?

Father was trembling. Though his trembling is not such as would be noticed by everyone. I can discern it easily. His face looks strange. I have seen him before with this face only once—on the day our shop had been sealed by the Corporation, and he had returned home tired after an arduous but fruitless day of search for money. I was frightened by his look and I had gone out of the house—the same we are selling away.

The expression on father's face is unchanging. Perhaps he is conscious of our presence. So far, we have had a house, and henceforth nothing will remain. Money will come, and he is a spend-thrift. The thought of my younger brothers comes to my mind. We are sitting here, while they must be busy vacating the house. Father has failed to arrange for another house, and now he is going home, our native village, with mother.

The fact is that he had no money, and you can't rent a house without a premium. I have been constantly with him for the last three months. In fact, he could not have been left to himself.

I look at the attorney's face. The expression on his face is always the same. I am reminded of a friend of mine as I catch him looking at me. His name is also Subodh. I frequently visit his home. I have also visited Subodh babu's during these three-four months. Father took me along to his house in the morning whenever he was in need of money. After a little chit-chat, Subodh babu would ask him to see him in the office. I would accompany father to his office in the afternoon. Father had borrowed quite a big amount in this manner, and now we have to pay an interest for the same at the rate of twenty per cent. And yet, Subodh babu's facial expression does not change.

I look appraisingly at the face of uncle Jagat. The blue veins in his thin hands look swollen today more than ever. He is glancing out the window. I have never had the nerve to look at his face. He had arrived only a few days before from the village. He has never done a thing in life. I have rarely met a person spoiling his life like him. Never a thing. And, if ever he gets any money, he simply drugs himself. I was thinking about the money he will get.

While thinking about uncle Jagat, my room flashes into my mind. The care with which I had decorated it! And the memories of so many people it is connected with?

Just then Subodh babu stretches the papers before elder uncle for his signatures. He is almost startled for a moment. Lost in himself, he had perhaps forgotten why he was sitting here.

He smiles as he signs. I am amazed. I have never seen him smile. I am gripped with a natural curiosity to know the reason of his smile.

'You have chosen me to be the first to be deprived of my right,' he says to the attorney in Bengali.

Subodh babu does not reply. Perhaps he is anxious to finish all this.

I look at father's face. He takes his spectacles from his pocket and puts them on. Recently he has minimized the use of spectacles.

He signs and moves the papers quickly away from him. We all look at him in surprise.

'You have got to sign at two more places. For Amarnath and Indranath.'

Amar and Indra! They again come to my mind.

'There ought to be a house, big or small, for every family,' Anand had said the other day, 'but these days people have no houses. Instead, they have rooms, roomlets, and sometimes nothing at all.'

What shall I have and what shall Indra have?

Father is wont to say, 'It's a universal law: if one laughs, another one will cry. One buys, the other sells.'

But why can't they all laugh together? Why is it necessary for one to cry to enable the other to laugh? Can it never be so?

Uncle Jagat has moved over and he is standing near father. He is watching him intently as he signs.

Presently, father lays down the papers before Subodh babu. Perhaps he has signed all the necessary papers. His face looks extremely exhausted.

Subodh babu examines the papers carefully, and then pushes those towards the buyer's attorney. Father is looking at them.

'It is all right,' the attorney says slowly as he examines them.

Uncle Jagat is still standing. Subodh babu asks him to sit down. A chair beside me is empty. He comes and settles down in it.

Subodh babu hands him the papers. Then indicates the space for his full signatures and initials.

Uncle Jagat looks at me. He hasn't got a pen. He doesn't carry a pen. Not only a pen, but nothing whatsoever.

I produce a pen from my pocket and put it in his palm. He sits on in silence. We do not speak either. A few minutes gone, Subodh babu asks him, 'What is the matter, why don't you sign?'

Uncle Jagat gives me back my pen. Then broods on for some moments, as if pulling himself to speak up.

'I don't want to sell the house. Where shall I live? I want a home'.

A soft smile comes to my lips. If father had not been present here, perhaps I would also have said the same thing.

'Don't be a fool!' Elder uncle trembles in rage, 'Are you on dope?'

'For the first time, I haven't taken the drug even though I had the money,' the lines in his face grow stiff.

There is an awkward silence in the room. None of us utter a word. Just then the telephone rings.

Subodh babu starts talking. From his conversation it appears that he wants to avoid an invitation to some party.

He smiles softly as he replaces the receiver.

Our eyes turn to uncle Jagat again. He is sitting quietly as before. I am afraid lest he walks out in a huff.

Just then elder uncle goes to him. Handing him a pen he says, 'Look here, it's not done like that. Already you have signed many a paper which expressed the desire to sell it.'

A faint tremor runs through him as he hears this. His face is blank. He adjusts the pen and signs up.

There is an awkward silence in the room. His flower-like little daughter's face flashes in my mind. I haven't seen her for years. My aunt—his wife—lives with her parents.

Uncle Jagat is the youngest among his brothers. Now it is the turn of the three sons of elder uncle. And then my two elder brothers and me.

Uncle Jagat has returned to the window. Subodh babu looks at Dharmanath bhaiya. He has been sitting there lost in himself. I had met him last night after seven years. It's because the house is to be sold that I am able to see him. Mother talks frequently about him. When young, he had mostly lived with his mother. He could never make up with his father. He did MA in Hindi some fifteen years ago. Promptly he got a job in a college. Two or three years later, he had married. He never came to Calcutta thereafter. Sometimes, he goes to the village to visit his mother. I had seen him in the village seven years before. He had enquired after my education, etc. Then he had asked, 'What do you want to be?'

'Everything', I had replied emphatically, and then had ran into the house.

Last evening I ran into him on the staircase. The steps are steeped in gloom since long. When the bulb fused, nobody replaced it.

I couldn't quite recognize him in the dark. I had gone out. He was talking with father when I returned home at nine. They had a long talk. I just listened. He had said with a laugh as he saw me, 'You have grown so tall, even taller than me. You'll surely become everything.'

I was reminded of my answer as I heard this. It was so surprising that he could remember such small things.

Bhaiya looks at all of us, one by one. I smile as I catch his eye. He doesn't smile. He gives a careful look at the papers. Then puts his signature and pushes away the papers towards Subodh babu.

'Please put your initials at these two places,' Subodh babu says in Hindi.

I am surprised. This is the first time I am hearing him speak Hindi. He always talks in Bengali with our family. I look at Bhaiya appraisingly. Perhaps Subodh babu has met him for the first time.

Bhaiya puts down his initials and returns the papers again. Subodh babu regards him for some moments.

'May I go?' Bhaiya gets up abruptly. We are taken aback.

'Won't you take your money now?' asks Subodh babu, again in Hindi.

'Money—you give him,' pointing to elder uncle. 'It is he who had bought it.'

Subodh babu thinks over. The attorney by him whispers something in his ear.

'No, please wait. I'll give you the money. You are free to give it yourself to anybody you like.'

Bhaiya walks up to uncle Jagat near the window. He says something softly to him, then glances out the window at the sprawling city.

After him, Bhaiya's two young brothers. They sign up mechanically. Perhaps everyone is fed up with it. Let it be over soon.

Why should I be the last, I wonder. Why didn't it happen a year before, or two years later from now! After two years, Amar would have signed in the end. And a year before, I wouldn't have been here. Then Bhaiya would have been the last. Thinking of this, I look at him. I call him Jai. You couldn't take him for my senior if you saw him. Rather, he looks two or three years younger than me. Subodh babu had said as much when he saw him, 'So you are the youngest!'

Everybody laughed or smiled at this. Subodh babu was embarrassed. Elder uncle had said, pointing at me, 'No, he is the youngest'.

'I am the youngest.' I repeat it to myself. Everything is incomplete without my signature.

Vijay Bhaiya is signing. I look at him as if I am seeing him for the first time. His hand quivers faintly as he puts his signature. I had apprehended this.

Vijay Bhaiya was most comfortable in this house. He may never again get a house like this. He is a clerk in a small firm. There isn't much hope for his becoming anything more. He had dropped out of the school after he plucked in the Matric. It evokes a curious pity in you as you look at him.

I look at him. I am afraid he would also say something like uncle Jagat.

Abruptly he gets up. Everyone except me watches him curiously. He flinches as he sees all eyes fixed upon him. He walks up to me and says softly, 'Give me a pen, my pen has no ink in it.'

I give him a pen from my pocket. I am sure his pen is full with ink. He stands up, as if to say something. But he loses the courage as everyone was staring at him.

Vijay signs in a deliberate manner of children who inscribe their names in the examination copies. We all watch him. He takes a lot of time.

The time is fast approaching. Vijay Bhaiya did not return my pen. But I have got another.

Vijay hands over the papers to Subodh babu. Subodh babu checks them thoroughly. Then, smiling at me, 'Fine? Now your turn, young boy!'

There is smile on the faces of half of the people present. Their smile would grow as I sign.

I do not pick up my pen though the papers are spread out before me. Suddenly I feel as if I will lose my senses.

For a moment I almost wished to run away quietly, to go wandering aimlessly in the streets, then slip into home at night and go to my bed. Home. But home is now a question mark. Suddenly my eyes fall on father's face. I recall the last three months and the agony through which he is undergoing.

Quickly I take the pen, and, slowly, sign up.

Subodh babu examines the papers. Then says slowly, 'Now?'

Now! And we all look up at him. 'Now you will all have to go to the police court. It will take only twenty minutes or so. Would you take your money now, or after returning from there?'

'Please give it now,' Dharmanath Bhaiya says.

We are all looking at him. Elder uncle regards him with affection. Perhaps he also wanted to say this, but couldn't.

Subodh babu had already prepared bundles of currency notes with names written over them. Those were kept in the bag of the buyer's attorney.

We climb down slow. An assistant of Subodh babu accompanies us. We have to go to the police court. I look around at everyone. Never again may so many of us come together!

The police court is crowded. We stand close to each other in the empty space. I think of my younger brothers and sisters, my mother, who must be waiting in the footpath with the household goods.

Suddenly Dharmanath Bhaiya tells Vijay Bhaiya, 'Houses are not only sold and purchased, they could be built, too. But how many people think of that.'

I recall what Anand had said, 'These days people have no houses. Instead, they have rooms, roomlets, and sometimes nothing at all.'

'It's nothing.' I say softly, and try to smile.

The Sahara

Sahara

Things in childhood are strange indeed! Our ecstasies over insignificant things in those days surprise us today. The way we used to be filled with immense happiness at reading or knowing about anything.

I was awarded a scholarship when I passed the middle. I had scored distinction in Hindi, georgraphy and maths.

Georgraphy was my real love. I had two books on geography and I knew them word for word.

And I remember the day when Masterji spoke about the Sahara during the period of geography: The Sahara is a great desert. There is nothing there except the sands sprawling far and wide. It is extremely hard to be traveling there. The sand-storms are so ferocious that nobody can survive.

I was all tears as I listened to him. Back at home in the evening, I hunted out the details on the Sahara. I was thrilled. I had been filled with a strange elation at the thought that I was born in Hindustan, and not in the Sahara.

'The midlands between the Ganga and the Yamuna are extremely fertile,' I happily read. All my days since my birth have been spent herein.

'Bengal is a lush green land. Calcutta is the greatest city in India.'

My father and various members of my family lived in Calcutta. And I was glad to be able to think that I could go and live in Calcutta, in the midst of the lush green Bengal, any time I pleased. Not the Sahara, but the fertile heartland of Ganga and Yamuna. The idea itself pushed me to the brink of a glowing dream.

However, soon a time came when the geography books vanished in the thin air, and I was suddenly an adult. I look back with envy at those days which could float me into ecstasies merely with the reading of a page or two of geography!

I had dozed off in the afternoon. When I awoke, I was soaked in perspiration. I felt a bit thirsty also. I wanted to call out to Pran who would have been studying in the next room. But just then I remembered that he must be in Esplanade at that house; may be knocking at the doors of the shops in Chowringhee, with a bag in hand.

The tin sheets are so hot in the summer. No season—winter, summer or rains—is comfortable in these rooms at the top of the roof. In summer, tin sheets heat up, in winter it is much colder, and during the rains, the space shrinks.

That day people had been so worried in the morning. The mercury was touching 104. I told them the thermometer could not be relied upon, as I had bought it for only twelve annas from a hawker in Chowringhee, yet they believed in the gadget, not me. Subhash was almost sobbing. Prakashji had suddenly made himself busy.

All of them were quiet. I had to say something. 'Prakashji, you go!' I said, contriving a faint smile. 'I am losing all the same, but why should you! It is just a common fever. I will ask Prem or Subhash to stay at home if it becomes necessary.'

Prakashji gave a look as if he had been awaiting my permission to leave. Subhash is the younger brother of Prakashji, and Pran, mine. Prakashji is about my age. Yet unconsciously they have collectively accorded me the status of a guardian.

It is about three o'clock. The thirst is growing. I feel too weak to get up from the bed. Pran must be going around the petty shops in New Market, Chowringhee and Lindsay Street. Subhash must be waiting in the classroom for the last period to be over.

I would rather not get up. I will ask for water when Subhash arrives.

Subhash did not want to go to the college today. I had sort of forced him. The look on Prakashji's face had been unbearable for the last three days. It is really surprising to witness a healthy man like Prakashji worried.

The examinations are almost over and his coaching institute is about to close. Last year also it was closed down during the vacations, but at that time some of his friends had gone away to the village, and so, he was able to procure some good tuitions. This year there was no such chance.

Prakashji hints at the difficulties he will have to face in the absence of a tolerably good job. I hear him in silence.

'Have you ever registered yourself in an employment exchange? I think, a regular work will suit you more than these occasional stints,' I tell him.

'I had registered myself about one and a half year ago. Not one call to date!'

'"Wanted" columns in the newspapers also could be helpful. I had been doing only that for months after the BA exam. Nothing ever happened. If only I had money, I could start some business.'

I look at his face. A little money is enough for business. A little land is enough for agriculture. Those who have neither, they are bound to look for a job. Wanderers in the desert have no morality. And it is always some invisible hand which determines whether you should get or miss a job! I recall the vivid description related by Masterji, long ago, of the search for water in the desert.

'I trust everybody. How else should I have given Mohanlal straps worth one hundred and fifty rupees on credit?' I say.

Aditya gives a soft smile. 'The question is not that of trust or mistrust, but of realizing your money. And you're unlikely to get back that money. I had even asked you one day to consult me whenever you lend any money to anybody.'

'But tell me, what am I to do now? It is nine hundred rupees. Still you will be gaining six hundred.'

My head reels. Despite my so many years in this line I cannot stand such talk. Aditya's smile broadens.

'You know I can never do that. You have known me for ten years. Who does not want to lead a pure and simple life? But where is the basis for that?'

I have no answer. My mind goes back to Prakashji. 'I had advised you years ago, don't sell the shop. Fill it with smuggled goods as others are doing. It will run on its own. You did not listen to me. And later on I have seen you wander in this very Chowringhee, with smuggled goods in your bag, I have seen you supplying to the shops.'

I keep silent.

'The system has gripped us. We are bound to do all that our heart rejects.'

I know he is talking rot, but it appears so true today. I find myself surrounded by fear when Pran gets angry. And a strange kind of fear. I feel guilty for all his troubles.

'I shall not do this work. It is in vain to wander day in and day out with the bag in hand. Why don't you get me a job by putting in a word to someone?'

Pran has passed Inter in second division three years ago. He couldn't continue his education and it pains me even today. Perhaps it would have been easier to get employment after BA.

'For some time you go away to the village. That will be a diversion as well as a boon to health. In the meantime I will see what can be done?'

He keeps silent. The expression on his pale face never changes. Only, there comes a mild quiver when one is angry.

I have spent hundreds of nights brooding about Pran. He is my youngest brother. I am simply drifting. Shall he too bear all this? I am startled at this thought.

Pran does not go to the village. Whenever I ask him to go there, he becomes restless.

On one of such days he even told me, 'Do you think anybody can enjoy being in a village? I do not know if there is anything there except murder, quarrel, starvation and litigation. Villages we have been reading about in the books are nowhere to be found in India.'

I keep silent. I think I'll ask Aditya tomorrow. His maternal uncle owns an oil mill. Maybe something will turn up.

Recently Prakashji has been very cheerful. He hopes to get a job in a private high school. He has had a talk with the secretary who has promised him.

These days he keeps talking until late hours in the night. Suggests an honours course for Subhash. Says Subhash could become at least a lecturer in a college after a good MA.

Often, when we are in a light mood, we talk about each other's marriage. Prakashji's father writes to him frequently from home, that he has selected a pretty girl for him. He doesn't respond to such letters. Even otherwise he rarely writes home.

He is going to be appointed to the job within the next eight or ten days. Everything is settled. Often he talks about the tuitions he would retain or give up after joining the school. Sometimes he advises me to get Pran enrolled in the third year. At least he could hope for a teachership after graduation.

There is happiness in his countenance, as if he has found water in his voyage in the desert.

But, no, it was not water. It was sand which looked like water.

It was hard even to glance at him that day. He had just been told that the post in the school had already been filled. The Secretary comes from Rajasthan. He got somebody from his native province, and forgot all about Prakashji. Shall this caravan of four keep wandering in vain? If you had an aim in life, you would do everything, somebody had told me. But I wonder if one could think of an aim in such circumstances! I get very few letters from my village. My father writes to me only when it is something urgent. But Pran gets letters frequently. He has a friend in the village who keeps him posted with all sorts of news about the village, from marriages to droughts to floods. I have never come across anyone who was ever happy to read a letter from his village. Time marches on. What is the destiny of us four? No joy has ever strayed into our lives.

'These days it is quite easy to get a clerkship in the Railways', Prakashji was saying the other day. 'Try for Pran. A boy from my village has just been recruited. There is a man in Howrah to whom you have to pay five hundred rupees. The rest, from the adjustment of the marks to getting through the interview is his job. You get nearly one hundred and thirty rupees a month in the beginning. What is the harm if one gives away just a four-month salary!'

Aditya seems to be right. Wanderers in the desert have no morality.

'It is not a question of five hundred rupees, Prakashji, but just think how bad one feels about it.'

'The heart revolts. Does not feel nice. Perhaps there is no room for such things in Calcutta any more. They call it cheap sentimentalism.' Prakashji's face is expressionless. As if it belongs to somebody who died only a while ago... The desire to lead a sound and pure life!

Masterji had told us: When the thirst grows unbearable, people slay the camels and drink up the water stored in the sacs in their stomachs.

And Aditya also had said the other day, 'Why are you rotting like this? You had better join us! There will be a regular income, and Pran can complete his course. I wanted to offer you this when you sold your shop, but you wouldn't have agreed. My business runs on the smuggled goods. I know you would agree now. The experience of three years of wandering should be enough.'

I am aghast. Aditya is so sure of himself. Perhaps my convictions are tired of themselves. Tired convictions cry for a rest.

How odd it is that even convictions get tired! Perhaps everything pertaining to our body tires out, and convictions after all belong to our being.

I am employed as the Manager of Aditya's shop. As if at last some muddy water has been discovered in the desert.

Sometimes I am surprised at the firmness of Aditya on his own ideas. Perhaps even a lie sometimes becomes so strong that it looks like truth.

Aditya still talks about the bygone days. The days when he used to visit our own shop. He was my friend. Had I followed his advice, I would also be the owner of a shop, like him.

Sometimes I feel I am not alone. Look at Prakashji! There are many people like me. They are a force. A force which is scattered.

And the other day, I was reminded of Aditya as I looked at the sick face of Pran. Aditya and Pran—the Sun and the Life. The meaning of these two names struck me and a melancholy smile descended on my lips. Only the sun can shine in a desert; life is bound to wither and wilt.

About fifteen years ago I had first heard of the Sahara. And how elated I was to think that I had not been born in the Sahara!

Today it all appears so silly.

Villain

Khal Nayak

I stopped still at the gate.

Everything looks just as before. Perhaps places and environment do not change as rapidly as we change.

It is startling. I must have stopped here out of sheer habit, just as I used to do years ago. I would walk in my natural brisk pace up to this point and then stop here abruptly.

I had not informed Meera about my arrival. I wanted to give her a surprise. How happy she would be.

There are children playing in the front side. There is Lily standing in the verandah, smoking a cigarette. Mr White is pacing up and down along with his black dog. I have to go to the back portion. It is incredible to see so much solitude amidst the madding crowd all around.

An old memory suddenly flickers. It aches. I had told Mummy, perhaps too somberly, 'Mummy, this is not a good place'. Mummy had stared blankly at my face. Those eyes have followed me ever since, wherever I may go. Sometimes I have been lost in the thought of Mummy and Meera for days on end, unable to do anything else.

Meera! I'll be meeting her exactly after one year.

I'd gone to my village for a day while returning from Kanpur. Mother had tried to persuade me in the evening, 'If you do not want to marry a girl of our choice, choose for yourself. Time never returns'.

Upon this, Meera had come to my mind. I recalled the evening three years before.

'No one can separate us.' I had finished the sentence hurriedly.

'No one!' She had echoed with enthusiasm...

Mummy smiles as she sees me. Seeta runs up to me.

'Where were you all these days? Years have passed. Meera misses you so much.'

'You know, Mummy, I wasn't here. Had I been, I'd have come every evening. Where is Meera?'

'She has not yet returned from office. Sometimes she is late. Sit down, I'll go make tea for you'.

'No, not now. Let Meera come'.

I feel the packet of cigarettes in my pocket with my fingers. I have never smoked in the presence of Mummy. I'll not smoke today either.

'Meera!'

I stand up with a jerk. Meera is standing before me in a light pink sari. I have never before seen her wearing a sari. Surprised and happy, she looks on at me.

'I'm not a ghost,' I say with a laughter. 'Sit down.'

'How do I know? You must find some other word for one who never acts like humans.'

'You have changed my name so many times, and now I must accept this new one, too.'

Her eyes are wet as she looks at my face. Her face shows fatigue of the day spent in the office. She had got the job just one month before I left Calcutta...

'Ain't you still there, I mean, with the same office?' I ask her after some reflection.

'This is my third job.'

The memory of an incident crossed my mind. She had joined a private institution before she joined the shorthand course at Young Women's Christian Association. A few days later she left it. When I asked her about that, she had told me with a little embarrassment. 'The atmosphere there is not good.'

'But you never mentioned this in your letters'.

She did not reply.

I have a mind to ask her about her salary but I drop the idea. I'll come some other day in the afternoon, and find out everything from Mummy.

Presently Mummy enters with two cups of tea for us. Also, biscuits in a plate. I beckon Seeta. She is sitting on a bed placed at some distance. Both Meera and Mummy love her immensely.

'She must be in fifth standard now?'

'No, in sixth', says Meera. 'She stood first in the fifth'.

Her eyes reflect deep affection.

Sipping the tea, I think that perhaps I should not have come at this hour. Meera must be quite tired and she needs rest.

'I'd leave now. I shall come later,' and stand up as I say this.

'Stay for a while. You haven't told us anything about yourself. How many days' leave are you on here?'

'I've quit the job.'

'Why?'

'Perhaps one cannot live all alone in a city like Kanpur for more than a year.'

'What will you do now'?

'Something. Anything. Here.'

'Isn't Umesh here?'

'Yes!'

'What's he doing?'

'Nothing much. He has some tuitions, etc.'

Umesh is my younger brother. I used to live with him and Anadi in Lake Gardens before I went away to Kanpur.

'I told you that you wouldn't like it there. Try to find something here.'

'Perhaps I won't go anywhere else now. I'll take up anything I can lay my hands on.'

There is a faint smile on her face. Perhaps she is happy at my decision. But, who knows...

I had taken the bus after some aimless wandering in Chowringhee. I have arrived here only this morning, but it seems as though I was here the last evening, even the day before yesterday, nay, even before that, every day.

Durban ji (watchman) is smoking his *hookah* at the foot of the staircase. When I lived here I always exchanged a few words with him at night, at whatever hour I returned. Today also I stop by him out of habit.

'Everybody home, *durban ji*?'

'Master babu has not yet arrived. Rakesh babu is there. Said he would stay overnight.'

I was happy to hear this. I had written to Rakesh before my arrival, and I had expected him at the station. In the morning, when I found Umesh alone at the platform, I had enquired about Rakesh. He said that Rakesh had suddenly gone to Titagarh on a company assignment. He would be back by the evening.

'Does Anadi return late every day?'

'Yes, not before ten o'clock,' he said reflectively.

I am climbing the stairs thinking about Anadi. I have never met a man who works as hard as Anadi.

Very slowly I climb the steps, lest others hear my footsteps. There are two rooms at the top. There is some open space where the steps end, and then the door to the flat.

I stop still at the door. Inside, they are talking about me. Once I used to be fond of eavesdropping. But today I don't want to listen surreptitiously. I give a soft rap on the door.

Rakesh is standing before me. My face fills up with smiles.

'I was missing you since the morning. I was wondering if we would meet today. You were constantly complaining in your letters that I do not visit Calcutta. Now, I have come back among you, leaving all that behind.'

'Have you resigned?'

'Didn't Umesh tell you?'

'I've arrived here only ten minutes before. I knew Umesh and you will be awake until four in the morning. I did not want to miss a long night of small talk.'

'Have you taken your dinner?' asks Umesh.

'No. In Chowringhee I did think for a moment to go and eat at Anarkali. But then I thought I had been eating alone for a whole year. Today I'll join you.'

Even today there is no firm arrangement for food, etc. Rather the same as before, when I too stayed here. There is a state bus garage nearby. And there are some Bengali restaurants around it. We used to eat mostly there. Sometimes we'd purchase *roti-tarkari* (bread and cooked vegetables) from the Janata Hotel and eat together at home.

'Let Anadi come; then I'll get *roti*s from the Janata Hotel for you,' said Umesh.

We had been talking late into the night after eating. Anadi had gone to bed early as he was tired. It was three or four o'clock in the morning before we shut our eyes.

Umesh had to miss two tuitions in the morning. Although Anadi woke him, he fell asleep again.

He was doing four tuitions at that time: two in the morning, and two in the evening. In spite of his best efforts he failed to obtain a regular job. He had been learning shorthand for the last three or four months.

Maybe he will get something after completing this course.

We had both gone out together in the evening. He got down at Bhavanipur while I went up to Esplanade. I must find some work for I don't want to leave Calcutta again.

I had arrived in New Market after a whole year. The familiar faces received me with tired and stale smiles. Whenever I come to New Market, I seldom go home without visiting Meera. But that evening I didn't.

The first month had gone by comfortably. I would meet Meera once or twice a week. Nevertheless, there was a strange melancholy growing every day.

In the afternoons, Anadi and Umesh were usually at home. Perhaps those moments made us feel our unemployment most acutely. Rakesh was with us only on Sunday afternoons.

Often *durban ji* would bring letters to be read out to him in the afternoons. He is from a village in the Sultanpur district. His family was in a very bad shape, and the landlord paid him only fifty rupees a month. His visits were quite painful for all of us.

One day I went to Roxy to see a film with Rakesh. After the show was over, We sat for quite some time in the Kalpataru. Rakesh's eyes were red. He weeps when he sees films. He told me once when I asked him about this. 'I don't know why, but I can't stop myself from weeping.'

He is quite sentimental. But in this film even I could not check my tears. It was a very long, sad, unsuccessful love story.

'Who was the villain?' Rakesh asks me broodingly.

'Villain?' I sit up. There was no villain in the film, indeed!

Villain?

That night I had been talking with Umesh till four in the morning. I had met Mr Bhargava in Dalhousie in the evening. He knows my father. He has his offices in all the big cities in the country. After a great many entreaties on my part, he had said, 'There is no vacancy at present in Calcutta. But we need a clerk in Lucknow. You may go there if you like'.

I had left a job in Kanpur. Shall I now have to go back to Lucknow? I couldn't say yes or no. I told him, 'I'll let you know tomorrow. Let me think over it.'

Anadi, when I asked for his opinion, said, 'You are wiser than me. Do as you like.'

Umesh advised me to accept it. He had said, 'It is very difficult to find a job in Calcutta. Who knows when this wait will come to an end?'

And, in the dark of the night, I had to reconcile myself to the idea of going away to Lucknow. I did not want to see Meera. I'd write her from Lucknow, I thought.

Rakesh, Anadi and Umesh had come to the station. The atmosphere was very heavy as they all knew that I was going away against my will. Each of us was trying to make the others laugh, but our jokes were not funny enough.

As the guard gave his whistle, Rakesh said, 'Hope to see you very soon.'

Before I could reply, the train pushed off. A long distance I sat thinking about Meera only. Just for once, the story of the film I had seen with Rakesh flashed in my mind.

I look out of the window at the sprawling darkness. Out there, there must be some villain, hiding in the vast darkness.

Villain!

Govind Mishra

Govind Mishra (born 1939) has authored more than 53 books that include collections of short stories, novels, essays and self-reflection pieces. He has been honoured with the most prestigious Hindi literary awards: Vyas Samman (1998), Sahitya Akademi Award (2008), Bharat Bharti Samman (2011) and Saraswati Samman (2013). Like in the works of his contemporaries, we find a new style of narration peculiar to him. His writing skillfully captures the state of the various sections of the Indian society.

The Beginning

Shuruaat

There he sat curled up busy scratching the ground.

Nearby lay the ant hills. Now and then he sprinkled mud over them. For a moment the ants would scatter only to form their train again. Those were the rainy days—the earth was damp and his hands were dirty. He was totally unaware of the surroundings and when I interrupted him, he gave me a startled look and then thoughtfully, as it were, he turned his eyes towards the sky.

What could he be brooding about...? I almost shuddered. That particular time, I would rather have him on the lawns. In fact, I should not have brought him here at all. Initially I was almost determined to put him only in an ordinary school. That was why I had left him with my mother. Even this time when I had gone to fetch him, I was glad to see him return home from school with my mother...he was running ahead with another boy, while I followed discussing his future with my mother. Hardly did he pay any attention to me. He galloped home through lanes and by lanes long before we reached. It was nice to see him grow in that small town just as I had grown. I was almost compelled to have second thoughts, as to whether I should really snatch him away from his world. Finally despite my mother's protest I did bring him to my wife; sending him to public school was the main consideration. Moreover—and this I could hardly put candidly—I didn't want him to be like me, a victim of lousy sentimentalism or some such thing. I do think I would have been as smart as other city-bred men had I not been brought up in that scraggy town.

We were new to both the city and the building. Every second person here wore horror on his face, even while waiting for the bus, each one seemed to be shrouded in the same mystique. In that building there were mostly officers, who bored themselves day and night in their one-roomed dens gloating over their status.

They hardly ever came out except when they had to really go somewhere. There was not much of mixing and whenever there was, it was within the confines of their quaint castle, hanging in the air of formality. There was hardly any room for the new. They were afraid lest the newcomer should pull from somewhere the taut skin of their tight faces and see them loose.

In the evening I took him to the lawn. Children of the building generally gathered there. Boys older to him were playing cricket. This side there were a few of his age too, who cut off from the main group were playing some systematic kind of game. I called them. They came close, their strong white legs flowing down their tight short pants. He should not be in such a baggy dress, I thought. 'What is your name, Mr...?' I asked one of them.

He pronounced his name looking at me rather curiously. Perhaps in that city he was not accustomed to such a thing or that kind of deep interest. 'And yours?' I asked the other one. He also pronounced his name and instantly turned towards his companion.

'Look here, this is Seelu...Seelu...this is... Now you all go and play together.'

I had pushed him forward. Having introduced them to each other I felt relieved. Now they would carry him hand in hand and shall play together every day like that... I thought.

They both simultaneously surveyed him from head to toe, threw a glance at me and then broke into laughter looking into each other's eyes...almost abruptly they fled back into their crowd.

The boys were rude—the public school type...I thought. What did he feel then? I felt as if an interview board had burst into laughter as soon as I entered and I have been rejected without having been asked a single question.

Next evening I made one more attempt. I took his football and asked him to come over to the lawn. He cried almost. 'I don't want to play,' he said. I persuaded him ultimately.

They must have been three then. I was alert this time to ensure that they do not run away again. I thought of beginning like this—'Come on boys, I'll tell you a game'. But this might sound like a song of Sehgal and they might run away. I assembled them at a place and also tagged him there. This time I wanted to begin with a game so that they would not stare at him and he could also be himself. 'Look here,' I said, 'you are four. You two hit the ball from this side and you two from that side.' They watched me strangely as I spoke in Hindi. I repeated the same thing in English also. This assured them at least about me. In fact, I was myself weary of my tutorial tone. But the game did start anyhow. I withdrew after a while. He was also beginning to take some interest. I felt relieved. Children are children after all. I slipped away as soon as I got the chance, to write some urgent letters.

When I came out again to have another look at them, I found him sitting at the end of the verandah, trying to draw something on the ground with his toe. The football was also lying there. I enquired about the boys. He murmured something. He looked terribly irritated with the environment as well as with himself. The boys must have gone away again and there could be various reasons...he did not speak English, his clothes were lousy; he didn't know the games they play, he didn't talk in the uncle aunty style... could have been anything, I thought.

For a diversion I took him for a stroll along the road, beneath the trees. All the time, however, I was feeling uneasy—he was being taken for a walk like the old or the sick.

There was no improvement in the situation during the next few days. We were on the ground floor of the building. Towards the evening boys and girls would come down the staircase noisily to gather in the lawn. He would sit on a chair or a bed—one leg dangling, his head tilted or else he would fold and unfold the bedsheet. At the most he half opened the door to peep out at the boys going and coming. I shuddered at this. He reminded me of the sickly parrot of *Kadambari* (the Sanskrit classic) who like him stared at the forest with awe. The only difference was that annoyance, fear and thirst which were on his face could not be separated one from the other. Thirst showing on his face...what he shall become, living in that loneliness day after day. School-going was not easy either, he must be lonesome there too... Sometimes I felt very much irritated and scolded him as to why didn't he go out and play at least in the evening... Why does he keep himself locked inside all the time? Children make friends quickly, I thought. Despite all that, first he would try his best to keep himself inside. When compelled, he would go out only to sit in the verandah or to stand in the gallery... his face turned to the window, he would look aimlessly here or there or would scratch the panes or frames of the window, anxious all the time to be called inside again.

I pitied him. I was realizing his limitations. But there was no solution. I felt I didn't know how to look after children. When I took him out for the evening strolls, he reminded me of a pet dog. And dogs either make friends with their ilk or they fight. Nothing was happening here with him in spite of successive attempts. And finally I almost gave up.

I made enquiries, all this time, so as to develop my own contacts which might get him some company. I was told that the children there went by their schools...I ought to put him in a school where most of the children from this building go, particularly children of his class. One of the occupants of that building suggested there should be a children's club...where the new ones could be introduced ceremonially, otherwise the children hardly get a chance to mix. What was more realistic was that children went by their galleries. Children of one row of four or five flats played in their own gallery. They hardly ever met boys beyond that. And since I was on the ground floor where the neighbouring rooms were unoccupied, there was no question of having other children around.

Thus, unless there was a flat available in one of the upper floors and the same was allotted to me, his loneliness was intractable.

And then, one evening when I returned home from the office I saw him plucking flowers in the lawn. A few steps away from him stood a girl, slightly older than him. Both of them were quiet. (Perhaps they had already been taught to behave). I was reminded of the somberness and silence of the grown up faces in the streets. The girl would pluck a flower, move out, arrange it in the bunch held in the other hand, and vanish again into the bush. He was also doing the same except that he didn't come out as often. I was all the more surprised because he hardly ever loved flowers. Nor had he been given any opportunity to develop such a taste. The face of the girl was blank. She looked lonely, sad...not even sad...only a certain kind of disinterest towards the world outside was there. It was terrifying to note all this in a seven year old face. Deliberately I passed by them. The girl watched me from the bush only. There was nothing in her eyes—curiosity, joy or anger—nothing. She busied herself soon. He, of course, ran to me, 'Daddy, see how beautiful they are!'

I joined him in his enthusiasm. It was nice to see that he was enjoying something after all. I talked to him about flowers. He didn't know their names. In fact I also didn't know the name of them all.

'Daddy,' he beamed in the same mood. 'She has invited me home for tea tomorrow. It's her birthday...'

He pointed towards her and blushed suddenly. I am sure he didn't know earlier what a birthday was. It was the first thing he had learnt in that city. The suggestion for a children's club flashed back on my mind. How could anybody ever conceive of such a regulated and mechanical thing as that for children!

Of course, except for giving him permission straightaway, I couldn't do anything else.

Gyan Ranjan

Gyan Ranjan (born 1940) is a noted Hindi novelist and a short story writer. Through his narratives, he has come to be recognised with what he considered as a new generation of middle class, about whose lives he wrote. Depicting the complexities of modern Indian society and problems arising thereof is his forte. He is also the editor of the Hindi literary magazine, *Pahal*, which publishes poetry, fiction, non-fiction, critique and essays, concentrating on issues of contemporary interest. In 2016, he was honoured with the Gyan Garima Honorary Award besides several others.

The Flunkey

Ghanta

Patrola is located deep in the heart of the city. One could get there walking past a tailoring shop, a cycle stand and a parking lot. It is an anonymous sort of a joint, though quite well known to the guardians of the law. It is there that our regular sessions had been initiated. It offered us something unique—peace and license, a perfect hide-out, a place which the gentry abhorred to associate itself with. And as for our own credentials as citizens, they survive merely as a thin bare bone. We could even be labeled the *avant-garde* of our age, for we are all uprooted, even though, in fact, we are only a bunch of lazybones who would hiss at each other, but never stir. We have imbibed the stillness of the dead. Sometimes the booze may succeed in kindling a little fire in us, but any such indignation would evaporate itself into thin air soon after a bout of noisiness. The booze does sometimes seem to transport us to a state of acute awareness. The moment of redemption then appears to have arrived and we feel as if we have finally seen through the humdrum. However, our unstirring limbs are ever under the spell of Sant Maluk Das, that high priest of lethargy, and so the humdrum continues. It looks almost impossible to break out of our Patrola way of life. Patrola has become our sanctuary. Out and away from Patrola, as we trudge towards our hovels, we no doubt visualize the dimensions of our vast city. And few people can claim that they know the city as well as we do. But my comrades hardly maintain any links with their wives, children, society or the world at large. They are not 'anti' as such, but are, in fact, their own natural selves.

Of all my comrades, I was perhaps the only one about whom the last judgement had yet to be passed and who was still manoeuvring between the two magnetic poles with ingenuity and caution. It looks as though I have acquired this trait of cunning for life, but at the moment I am not quite sure.

So, often it happens that, when my health is in a bad way and I have sleepless nights in succession and notice that gentility is thriving without any hindrance, I then wander about the market, gazing at the show-windows, drink Coca-Cola and give a slip to my hello-hello Patrola. Maybe, my comrades also notice this, but they couldn't care less. I have even a few clothes totally incompatible with my personality and my Patrola way of life and they almost transform my appearance when I wear them, which I do only when I run away from Patrola. True, these 'costumes' are at times embarrassing, yet I have not discarded them altogether.

One day, as I went up to the *paan* shop outside the Patrola, I ran into Nem. It was rather late in the evening. He looked quite impressive now that he had become an insurance agent. At one time, he had almost joined the Patrola gang, but was saved by a stroke of luck. Happy and secure, he now envies our Patrola life. He grumbles, 'If only I had not been trapped in this bloody insurance business!' I believe he has enough money and comforts. A few minutes later, he was talking about Kundan Sarkar. This, too, was a permanent fixation with him and I was awaiting it. He ardently wants me to meet his Kundan Sarkar.

The issue had been hanging fire for years. This time Nem even promised me, with a certain slyness, liquor at Kundan Sarkar's. He assured me that I would not get bored with him. 'You are a writer and he is an intellectual. A perfect pair you will make!' To be honest, I had bid good-bye to literature ages ago, although perhaps a few crumbs of it still clung to me. But I kept this secret to myself. I knew it was a sheer waste of time to argue with him. Ṇem is a perfect burr. Walking away, he shouted, 'Don't you shirk! Tomorrow! You can't find another man so unassuming, so friendly. Tops! What else do you want, brother!' Halting again, he said somewhat excitedly, 'He would even go with you to a *houli* for a drink. He is not finicky at all. So then, tomorrow!'

I went back to Patrola just to fortify myself before the fated encounter. My sole aim was the free booze and I was chanting, 'Kundar Sarkar, Kundan Sarkar'.

His is a formidable name. A sheet-anchor to all sorts of writers and intellectuals, mostly from the middle-class, who are wont to sing paeans to their benefactors. A mere glimpse of the man would bring an irrepressible itch and a blissful tickling just where the ape shed his tail and became man. He carried an aura of awe around himself which they had bestowed on him. Without telling my comrades anything about him, I quickly stole away from Patrola. In fact, I could not have confessed my greed for the booze before them. In any case, the Patrola gang cared two hoots for people like Kundan Sarkar. They were thoroughly convoluted. Only I vacillated, still beguiled by things like respectability, status, money, country, nation, society and so on.

Kundan Sarkar held a post at a place where it was usually difficult to mix with common people. And yet he was sociable in a unique way. He managed to dupe the hierarchical norms. He was just crazy about literary gossip and ran after connoisseurs and intellectuals, inviting them to booze with him. There were hundreds of such artists and writers in the city, but Kundan Sarkar was not daunted by numbers. He always kept one of them with him, just one at a time. He was experimenting. And whoever accompanied him at the moment was branded his *ghanta* or flunkey.

So, now, I was the *ghanta* of Kundan Sarkar. He just took me in his stride. My feet wore the dirt of the streets and indeed I must have looked grotesque, yet it did not matter to him. I had a nagging doubt that I would perhaps be a misfit at his place. But greed is irresistible. Booze was the beacon of my life. Pinching a little liquor out of someone was, in my mind, almost a great feat of cunning.

Initially, he offered me a cheap booze, though I knew he must have had enough stock of expensive brands. Perhaps he first wanted to size up this intellectual. Besides, I was a man in tatters. Had I been as respectable as he was, Kundan Sarkar would certainly have accorded me better reception. On the contrary, my company seemed to lure him more towards the rut of vagabonds and he would often coax me to take him to cheap joints.

In my company he would even refuse to hire a rickshaw when we were exhausted from wandering in the streets. For days on end, there would be no 'gainful programme' except for tea and coffee. One after another, he would smoke away all my bidis even when he was stocked with expensive imported cigarettes. What did I gain from this! Yet, I don't know why I went along. On his part, he was out to gather experience, to have fun and fulfillment.

Had I ditched my comrades just for this sort of enlightened stultification! Kundan Sarkar would vouchsafe off and on, 'Oh my! I have never have had such fun, such free life as this!' Never had such fun, you sonofabitch! You have come to me to seek fun!—I would grumble, touched on the raw. I longed for a chance to make mince-meat of this sham—both his and mine. I felt ashamed, too. I had come hunting for orgies, leaving my comrades in the lurch, and this was all I got!

My comrades never deflected from their hazardous life. They were firm and unrepentant. Only I was tormented, for I had become Kundan Sarkar's *ghanta*. But finally, I made up my mind to put an end to this state of dilemma. The moment of truth has arrived and soon it will all be over, I assured myself.

I had realized that it was not easy to keep up with Kundan Sarkar, and besides it was unnecessary. You could pull on with him only so long as you had the audacity to talk literature at least for two hours a day. In the beginning, I had not realized this mania of his, for literature troubled him like piles. However odd a situation and whatever the mood of conversation, he took only a nonce to veer it towards literature, just as one changes gears. I lacked such a *sadhana*. My insides creaked. The moment of truth is unavoidable, I told myself and, in any case, I had had enough of it.

Once Kundan Sarkar had pontificated at length that an artist ought to live as if on the brink of death. Only then can his coffers be filled with experience. He had an endless list of names who had squelched all their rivals. His utterances on literature were so bizarre that I felt like breaking my own head. He would say: 'Society is like a field, life is like manure, writer a farmer and literature the crop—just as woman is the earth, man a plough and progeny the fruit.'

I had to mumble something or the other, for reticence would give me away. He must not catch the wind of my exasperation, or else he would bundle me off even before I took a pot-shot. So I went on chewing the cud ostensibly with relish. 'You have a wonderful tongue,' I would tell him. 'Wonderful?' he would flare up. 'You call reality a wonder! Bless you!'

He would often assert that he worshipped truth. 'Now, look here, I can afford to drink scotch, yet why do I drink hooch? Why do I smoke bidis? Why do I loaf about in the streets? Why do I wear coarse khadi? Why do I walk instead of driving out in my car? I am not even a writer, a mere intellectual. As a matter of fact, I find reality beautiful and I am garnering the gems of truth!'

At last the long-awaited day arrived. Catarrh had shaken me. My nose ran like a water tap. I was irritable. My cold was very severe on that fateful day. And, curiously enough, on that very day, he was going to be most generous to me. He was spending money with both his hands. From morning till evening, we wandered about drinking incessantly. I was determined to fleece him as much as I could, for it was going to be the last day with that nanny. When it grew dark and the lights went up, he took me to a restaurant. I had never been there before. It was too genteel a place for me to step in. I get worked up in such places and feel like retching. But that evening, my body was suffused with exhilaration like a honeycomb full of honey and I swayed like a tree in strong winds without, however, getting uprooted.

The hall was full and the light was dim. Men and women were in equal numbers. The place was steeped with all manners of fashionable scents and with each turn of your nose to right or left, you had a different smell. Kundan Sarkar found a table with two chairs for us. He had a nip of gin in his jacket. As soon as we sat down, he began to grope for something in the semi-dark. I felt trapped. Gradually my breathing improved and I started garnering bits of information alertly. I had never before seen so many men and women together in such a place. My brain was turbid with hooch and catarrh, and yet I was quite alert. All of a sudden, I found myself gripped with the thought of our poor Mother India.

Kundan Sarkar told me that mostly army officers and their families visited that restaurant. I was instantly convinced that the people sitting there could only be army officers. It seemed a place with no links with the real world of my acquaintance. Nobody here looked irritable, sombre or sad. They all wore healthy, chubby and smooth faces. Kundan Sarkar also seemed to belong to this wholesome world. Anyway, how can you banish him from this world merely because he had condescended to have a drink in the company of a destitute!

I noted that there were two types of ladies in that hall. Some looked made of feathers while others gave the impression that they must be excreting by the buckets every day. Flatulent women devoured the males with their eyes. Men did not lag behind, either. Savouring various dishes, they were, at the same time, licking the honour of others' women in a highly civilized manner. To them, everyone else, except themselves, was non-existent. Perhaps they were also bugged by the idea that the hall provided just the right atmosphere for it and that the world was essentially created for their own sake. I loathed them for their slavishness and loathed myself who was nothing but a beast of burden in their eyes.

By now, Kundan Sarkar had uncorked the bottle between his legs and poured it into our half glasses of water under the table. Thus there was gin on the table, indistinguishable from water, and he was sipping it slowly. Just then the orchestra on the dais struck the first note. It was as though jackals were baying. Rather a bit too much of hocus-pocus. The cacophony of the orchestra bowled me over. I wanted to do something before I too fell in the groove and began to relish it in spite of all my spleen. For, no sooner you wish for a moment of respite than the world begins to thrust itself down your gullet. No, I don't want to swallow; I want to puke. The booze had saved me. Otherwise, I knew I would have been grinding my teeth and gone flat after that. Instead, I was filled with a rebellious gaiety.

I noted that I had improved upon my usual stilted smile which was my stock response in all such situations. This vegetarian smile is quite harmless to the establishment. Only a king, a *mahant*, a woman or those whose paradise is secure, can have a smile that carries force. For me, after the smile came nausea—it is a nuisance. However, it no longer ran its full course, for the romance of democracy and civic sense have been hammered so well into us that the impulse of subversion is smothered, leaving a mere lukewarm simmering in its wake.

Swiftly I lifted my glass and drained it. I was afraid lest the nausea, anxiety and spleen should leave me, the erstwhile smile supplanting them. One must nip the smile in the bud. I side-glanced at Kundan Sarkar: This is my last day with you, I will not be your *ghanta* hereafter, Kundan Sarkar! But how would he know that? He was drinking smugly. There was no dearth of people willing to play his *ghanta*.

Kundan Sarkar looked at his watch, ordered the bearer to get us something to eat and told me in a hushed tone, 'It's time. The girl will come up now to sing.'

'Okay, let the girl come,' I said.

Kundan Sarkar poured out the last drops from the bottle and I adjusted my chair to sit facing the dais, as if a film was about to be shown. There was the head of a woman, as big as a flowerpot, and black, blocking the view and so I had to adjust my chair again. Meanwhile, a few strong and handsome goons appeared, took two rounds of the hall and went back somewhere inside. Presumably, they were on duty. At first, I thought they were looking for someone, but, no, they went back quite self-importantly. Just like the troops parading on the streets 'for the benefit of the people'.

Instantly, a girl stormed into the hall. Rather than walking, she seemed to be floating in the air. She displayed her face before she climbed on to the dais and threw a kiss at everyone, like paper-planes floated out by children. With a petal-fresh face, she looked a little girl. A tight *kameez* of gold clung to her torso. She began to sing, swaying and swinging. You could see it from her eyes and her breasts that she was a pretty bitch.

The restaurant was a picture of refinement and taste. People sank back in their sofas and talked in hushed voices. I don't think they ever opened their traps wider than the size of goats' droppings. Perhaps the menfolk took the singing girl for a two-penny whore excluding their own womenfolk from that category. In their mind's eye glimmered the bed-room scenes. They were trying to impress upon their wives: 'Look, there are also other things besides you.' But, women, on their part, wouldn't give in either. They seemed to retort: 'Ah, darling! Look over there, that young man by the blue georgette. What a smart guy!' The husband seemed to snigger: 'He's not yet a Squadron Leader. He's just a junior.' 'So what! He is smart and handsome, and he will be more so when he becomes a Squadron Leader.'

At some distance from us, at the third table, there sits a middle-aged man, sporting long, needle-sharp moustaches. He thinks he is hoodwinking the onlookers, for while pretending to watch the orchestra, he tickles the cheeks of the women sitting by him with the point of his moustaches.

As I sat watching, I noticed grotesque things happening to the singing girl. The cord with which she had tied the *salwar* round her waist came down dangling between her legs. It looked soiled in contrast to her transparent tinsel dress. The cord also swung with the music. I burst out with laughter. I could not just control it. She now looked like a hussy. The sight was simply revolting, more so to the so-called civilized eyes. Kundan Sarkar was taken aback. He was conscious of the surroundings and winced at my laughter. His kind of consciousness fortifies you against everything, protects you in all contingencies. Kundan Sarkar scowled at me: 'Behave yourself. This is a high-class place. Did you find anyone else laughing at the cord?' Etiquette demands of the people sitting here that they feel as if their own cord had come loose! He tried to overawe me: 'Perhaps you think you are sitting in Patrola or what!'

'Hey, you shut up!' I could not restrain myself and I stood up. He had named my Patrola! I snatched the Coca-Cola bottle and held it by the neck. Presently, he began to cajole me: 'My friend, you are high. I'll order some lime-water for you.' He persuaded me back into my chair. It was the first occasion when he had come out with the characteristic jargon of his class, and the hollowness told. Anyway, he had successfully smothered my precious laughter.

I kept my seat as if I was alone and Kundan Sarkar sitting opposite to me was merely there like a piece of furniture. I had gone to Kundan Sarkar for the sake of booze, not to listen to a bully-tongue lamenting over literature, or to get my brains molested. But it takes more than ordinary human guts to put up with Kundan Sarkar.

A peculiar cocktail of remorse and anger raced in my veins. There was goody-goody humiliation all around. Instead of pluck and anger, only emptiness and loathing. Roaring darkness is enveloping me. Hammer blows resound in my ears. Presently, I saw myself addressing the august gentry gathered there. 'Look here, you military mosquitoes and butterflies, the time is not far when all this politeness of yours will have blown you over. You will be left holding your hands. You are going to lose your guns—they are not meant to fill your belly. Run! Run for your life!'

Eh, ten years of my life. Once it used to be nausea, followed by smile; now it is the other way round: first smile and then nausea. The same drudgery goes on and on and on. Just look at these well-oiled robots pocketing fat chunks of salary in the name of their country! And this slut from a slum, showing herself as a music queen. As if the whole country was just waiting to be rammed into her! Young faces reeled before my mind's eyes, those who had given up everything just for a puff of hashish. But the road of hashish led nowhere.

The hall is growing restive. Those sitting there, did they too, feel trapped? With a certain delight, the thought jolted me into a reverie. Perhaps I was coming into my own. The orchestra threw up a sluggish whir. The girl seemed to be drowning in a drowsy rhythm.

This is the last chance, I told myself. If you let slip this chance, the same old humdrum would take over again. Suddenly my fists clenched. Kundan Sarkar tried to stop me. He must have been eyeing me closely, but by that time the Coca-Cola bottle had escaped from my grip and there was a resounding bang. The front glass wall came crashing down. The girl fled from the dais. She yelled 'Police, Police!' and fell in the lap of a goon who had suddenly emerged from nowhere. Kicking the table away, I stood up and began to shout orders like a commander: 'Get out of here or...you will get crushed.'

Finally, when I came to, I found myself at the receiving end. Three or four goons were shuttling me from one to the other. One of the goons yelled at the onlookers and asked them to get back to their seats. Yet another escorted the frightened singer on to the dais, deploying himself by her side. He picked up the uselessly dangling cord and thrust it back to where it belonged. The chief goon who was supervising my bash-up was being addressed as Kallu Guru. They removed the splintered glass and me, just as they clear the wreck after an accident. A parting kick from Kallu Guru sent me flying near the door. I looked about for Kundan Sarkar for help, but he had vanished. I even called out, 'Kundan, Kundan'. But the name of Kundan enraged Kallu Guru even more. My jaws were dripping with blood.

Feebly, I clutched at the leg of a table to raise myself up. It was occupied by an extremely polite and frightened man who was perhaps praying for riddance. He whispered to his woman: 'He looks like a loafer?' But the lady was daringly cheerful and kept grinning at me.

I was not prepared to take any more kicks on my ass. Quickly I got up and hurried down the steps. I distinctly remember that I was somewhere midway on the staircase when the orchestra upstairs struck up again. Within three or four minutes, civilization was back on the rails. Downstairs, the guard opened the gate and clicked a salute to me. Poor chap! How could he know that this customer was a persona non grata, not worthy of such greetings?

And so a flunkey of Kundan Sarkar had fallen by the roadside. I was like a cyclist unhurt after a fall in a crowded street. Walking into a deserted alley, I found all my revolutionary fervour had gone. My nose blew with catarrh. Back home, in the dear old Patrola, comrades received me with an amused guffaw. Beyond that, they didn't seem to care.

Prayag Shukla

Prayag Shukla (born 1940) is a Hindi poet, art critic, translator and fiction writer. He has been honoured with the Sahitya Akademi Award for Translation, Sharad Joshi Samman and Dwijdev Samman, etc. He belongs to that lineage of poets like Raghuvir Sahay, who have produced unusual Hindi short stories in terms of thematic angles, sensitive handling of the language, and humane perception. He is popular among children too, as their writer.

A Friend in the Street

Sadak Ka Dost

Now as he looks back, he finds it all rather opaque. Yet, what comes out distinctly even now is that when after the lessons his tutor leaves him, he picks up some book and gets his wheel chair moved out in the verandah. Seated there, he looks on at the long street stretched in front of him with its occasional passers-by. And then, fed up with it, he glues his eyes into the pages of the book in hand. Sometimes he hears elder brother humming a tune from some English film, a tennis-racket swinging in his hand. He'd merely throw a glance at his room and walk away. It feels strange.

He straightens his back and starts looking at the tea stall across the footpath.

A thumping sound from the staircase. Usually it is his sisters and their friends coming in. A giggle as well, if it is audible. That's Leela. Yes, only she laughs so loudly. When Leela had come to this house for the first time, and had found him sitting in the verandah continually at the same place she had remarked to sister, 'What a lazy boy!' But when sister told her the whole story about him, she deeply regretted her remark. She had come up to him and said, 'I'm sorry!'

And he had just smiled quietly, pained.

Usually it is Bhabhi who brings him his breakfast. Mother rarely comes. Earlier, she used to come quite frequently. When Bhabhi comes and sits near him, she always tries to strike a conversation. Sometimes she even sings him a song. And she always wonders aloud: How do you manage to retain so many things in your mind just by reading or hearing them once!

Mother, if at all she comes, intones only this: 'Whenever you see him you find he is reading'. Or, 'Have you never seen a street before?... Just goes on watching it.... You will spoil your eyes, too!'

He swallows even this 'too' quietly.

Sometimes he wonders how he has survived these fifteen long years! Did he idle it away sitting in this chair and crawling with it in the rooms and verandah? Yes, he has visited Delhi twice, for treatment, in his fifteen years of life. That is about all... Sometimes he chokes with a lump in his throat as he thinks of his long acquaintance with the street. And then again, with a great amazement he fixes his eyes on it.

During the last few days he has found enough to keep himself occupied. The footpath on the other side of the street is overflowing with the people. It looks like a museum of antiquated and worn-out things, torn and old clothes, sacks, firewood, broken utensils... Children gaze at the sky. They beg alms of everyone passing, beating their own belly with their hands like a drum. There are women also, quarrelling, fighting and shouting. A host of mud-stoves are lit up at dusk. Flames leap up. And, much more.

Somehow, his eyes keep turning, time and again, in the direction of a boy sitting under the tree near the lamp-post. Silent, he looks like a stone idol. There is always someone to look after him. If the belly-beating urchins succeed in getting something, they bring it to him as a matter of course. The boy sometimes breaks into a song, in an anguished voice, and at such times passers-by stop still, and the footpath dwellers make up a circle round him. At night a woman comes and feeds him with her own hands, maybe it's his mother...

Bhabhi has come to know of this. Rather, he himself had told her.

'Look, Bhabhi, that boy is also like me.'

Bhabhi saw that a boy was sitting under a tree as she looked in that direction. There were several boys surrounding him. One of them was offering him something to eat. Bhabhi understood everything, yet she asked him casually, 'Why, so what?'

'Nothing,' he could utter only this.

That day Bhabhi sat for quite a long time with him. Perhaps Bhabhi also recounted this to mother. And mother told father. And in the evening, abruptly father had asked him, 'Why do you brood about them? Let them go to hell!' Father had been talking about a lot of other things. 'They will make it impossible for us to live here... It didn't take even four days to spoil the street, the footpath, everything!...Today they even broke into the garage and started pawing the car... Vagrants!... Refugees!'

It was a Sunday. Everybody was gone to an afternoon film show. He does not go anywhere. How difficult it is for him to move about. He had got his chair placed in the verandah. The sky was quite clear. He felt pleasant in the sun around four-five o'clock. But, all of a sudden the sky was overcast with clouds. Cold wind began to blow. In this place, clouds often gather just like that at any time. But he kept sitting in his chair. After a while the scene changed. Huge drops of rain began to fall. He saw a great hustle and bustle, almost a stampede on the footpath. They were all fleeing, young and old. Two men lifted the boy who was sitting under the tree and placed him under the shade of the verandah. He suddenly noticed that he was soaked... Oh!... There is no servant at home! He called out two or three times. But his voice was lost in the din of rain. With one hand, he tried to move the wheel, but the wheels got stuck just after a few turns.

He was still trying to get it moving when Ramu appeared, gasping, and moved the chair swiftly inside the room. Daubed his body with a towel and changed his clothes. Then he said moanfully, 'Babu, please don't tell mother! I am a poor man! It will ruin me, Babu, please!'

'No, no! Don't worry!' He had assured Ramu. And then, he had no control over his wild thoughts. Must he stick to this life, yet? Is it a life, anyway? They all go to the club, to the cinema, wear new clothes everyday, but he?

Then he began to muse about the urchin. Suppose that boy has no home of his own, no clothes, he... Musing, he fell asleep.

When he woke up, he found Bhabhi standing near his bed, quite worried. She was saying, 'Oh! Prem is in high fever!'

In comes mother, father, sister too. But gradually they all depart. Brother will go to the club to dance. Father too to some other club. Mother and sister will go out shopping!... How much do these people wander about! They have just arrived, and presently they will go away again. They will put on newer clothes. They will fetch more commodities.

For many days he was bed-ridden with high fever.

This morning he felt all right. He got his chair laid in the verandah. But he had a queer feeling as soon as he reached there. The front footpath was empty. That boy was not there under that tree. Instead another beggar sat there... Where have they all gone?

After a while Bhabhi appeared and said, as if she knew everything, 'They have gone away!'

'Where?' he asked.

'I don't know! One day some police vans had arrived. They were all evicted.'

'All evicted?' he whispered in a deep anguish. He felt as if he had lost a friend from the street. And he looked on aimlessly at his own legs that looked scorched and half of an almost dried up forearm.

Layers

Tahen

There is no sign of the train as yet. Why have they closed the gate so early?

The sky is thick with clouds. And though it had stopped raining an hour ago, the streets are still sloppy. How strong is the wind! And look at the fingers, numb with cold.

Niranjan takes out a bidi and lights it up. Then he looks at the railway quarters along the level crossing. As he closely watches through a window, he finds an old man, sleeping—in fact, not exactly sleeping, but coughing, lying on a charpoy with his back to the roof. A sense of isolation fills Niranjan with a kind of restlessness. The city has been left far behind. Even the villages and houses are few and far between. He finds it all out of order... an overcast sky and isolated looking places! He takes a deep puff.

'Why have they closed the gate so early?' asks Banshi, one of the two labourers sitting by him, with a puff at his bidi.

'I don't know but the train should be coming.'

'Perhaps, it'll rain again,' interrupts Nanku, the other labourer.

'Let it,' says Niranjan as he throws away the stub and produces another bidi out of his pocket.

With a deep puff at it he starts humming a tune, the bidi pressed between his fingers.

Nanku and Banshi have nearly finished their bidis.

'Want more?' he looks at them.

'No, Drebher Saab,' they say even though they had finished quite a few bidis while he was driving.

It is only a few days since Niranjan has started driving. That is why a kind of restlessness often fills him. His heart palpitates with apprehension. Perhaps, the apprehension will disappear over the days. Perhaps, then he will not feel so uneasy driving through the rain and storms.

'It's coming at last,' says Banshi and wipes his face with a rag.

'Yes, it's coming, a goods. My goodness...a goods train is never-ending,' says Niranjan.

Slowly the train approaches. Then stops close by, washed in the rain, wagons dripping, there are streaks of water.

'What happened?'

'Perhaps a 'passenger' will pass. It appears there is one coming.'

Whistles of the 'passenger' are distinctly audible.

Suddenly Niranjan notices three or four boys emerge out of nowhere, or maybe from the huts on the left. They have gathered near the engine.

The engine is hissing. It is so strange! Or, maybe it seems strange to him alone.

Banshi and Nanku are sitting pretty, with no concern for the world at large.

'These boys...my goodness! Gleaning coal in a stormy weather as this!'

Banshi bursts out laughing at Niranjan's comment.

Niranjan is restless again. It seems he won't be able to get along with this work—perhaps he won't be able to drive a lorry. He is not a professional as yet, not accustomed to such sights amid such weather. ...These boys have nothing else to do! They don't have to go to school?...nothing to do! But, who cares... Niranjan broods.

The city has been left far behind. Everything here looks so helpless—fields, houses, all under this dirty sky.

Niranjan throws away the bidi and rubs his palms. The lorry will have to be taken across after the goods-train has passed.

The goods-train hisses and chugs forward. The boys run away in all directions...barefoot, through the slop.

Niranjan starts the engine as the gate is flung open. In passing, he throws a glance at the old man with his back to the world. He seems hardly bothered by the rain or the storm. He must usually be lying like this and one fine morning this charpoy will be found vacant... Uh, what wild images.

With a little jerk the lorry thrusts forward. What kind of a road is this beyond the level crossing! So narrow! Tiled houses and hutments on either side are almost eating into the road. There is no vehicle in sight though if one of such things were to emerge all of a sudden, it's going to be terrible.

Why as a driver should he think like this! He was the star of the training school. What didn't he learn?... But it is not a training school lorry running on a narrow street. Niranjan broods, mutters something, and becomes restless again.

Huchch...oh, god! There are ditches full of water. He will have to be very careful.

The sky thunders. Darkness appears to have thickened. From where are all these clouds coming out rolling! Perhaps, another downpour is in the offing. Why is this road so narrow?

It seems there is nobody to look after these things. Scenes of the offices relating to these matters conjure up before him...

almirahs cluttered up with god knows how many registers... applications and complaints gathering dust in the files...and apparently nothing ever moves there. Thunder again! The city left far behind. The wind grown stronger.

'What a cold,' says Banshi. 'Ye!' Nanku affirms and ties the rag round his ears.

Before laying the road nobody would have cared to consult a driver as to whether he'd be able to drive it or not! And even when this road is now strewn with potholes, nobody cares to ask a driver about his difficulty in driving. The houses are literally smothering the road. The road, which'll remain tied down between rows of houses up to eternity...muses Niranjan.

He has been condemned to drive a lorry only because he could not go beyond matriculation...Huchch...

A curse for the road escapes Banshi's lips. It goes into his head. He has got to tag his each remark with a swear, just like other drivers. Perhaps, he'll soon fall in line with them. After all, how long can a man endure adversity in silence...Perhaps, you feel light once you have given vent to your suppressed feelings.

The very thought makes Niranjan restless again. Again emerge there what appear to be some houses by the road. No... not houses, they're shops where he might get some tea! Niranjan cheers up.

Why would anybody foul one's tongue if the roads weren't so narrow and ridden with holes? He grins as he thinks he too can think sense! 'Park it aside!' exclaims Banshi, 'Right on the edge, or else you'll have to rush back if a carriage comes this way.'

Niranjan parks the lorry, pushes the door open and gets down. The road is sloppy.

Banshi and Nanku also get down. The three enter a tea shop. Niranjan looks around wearily.

'Three teas!'

The walls of the shop are char black. The monotony is relieved by some calender cut-outs. There are one or two old and faded calendars also.

An old man is lying on a bench here too, a wiping rag under his head. There are also two or three other men.

Does this boy know what is the date? Niranjan asks himself. No, perhaps he doesn't know. The boy is straining tea into the glasses.

'Please!'

Niranjan takes the glass and has a sip.

'Drebher Saab, give us bidis now.'

He extends the bundle to Banshi and Nanku. And lights one for himself.

'What should be the time like?' he asks Banshi.

'Around two or two thirty.'

He does have a watch, but it is out of order.

They have got to cover some twenty miles more. It is going to be terrible until this narrow street ends. There's thunder again. He longs to go on sitting here, sipping the tea.

'Shall we go, Drebher Saab?'

He pays and comes out of the shop, throws a glance at the shops around...small shops, as if sprouting out of the slush. The same weary and withered walls...this narrow strip of a road will remain bound up forever among these shops!

Niranjan starts the lorry. How dark has it grown even though it's only two o'clock. God knows for how long the clouds will last. Small shops look even more dwarfish in the dying light...

A road ahead cuts across the one Niranjan is driving on. Near the crossing, some men and women are moving, literally hopping to avoid muddy pools.

'Banshi,' says Nanku, 'I'm hungry.' He opens a small bag and mouths the first palmful of *laai* (puffed rice).

'Huh!' a sound escapes Niranjan's lips. There are two or three cows ahead, the sound of horn fails to deflect them. He tries to avoid them.

'Hai... Hai,' shouts Banshi.

But the van hardly picks up speed when a man with two small girls appear in the middle of the road. The approaching lorry doesn't concern them. Niranjan presses the horn. The man gives a start and drags the girls aside. One of them is crying, maybe she had fallen down, her frock is soiled... To Niranjan everything appears besmeared in mud.

A village appears close by. It looks rather isolated under the clouds. Niranjan recalls the shops left behind. Lorries halting there and that boy serving them tea. Suppose the lorries stop taking this road! Then perhaps he will also join those coal gleaners at the level crossing. Perhaps the boy ardently waits for the lorries. The very thought that there are some shops in such a forlorn place pleases Niranjan. But how small and helpless were they looking.

There appears some van at the turn ahead. He straightens himself up in the seat. It is for the first time that he is passing through this narrow road with a loaded lorry.

The van is approaching. Nanku and Banshi are also peering over the wind screen. Quick, a bit faster, avoid that pit, says Niranjan to himself. Huchch... O God! Shall I be able to make it safely? Who knows if the road ahead is not worse!

The driver of the approaching van also has slowed down. The vans almost brush past each other.

Suddenly his wife's face looms before his eyes. She lives in the village. Now that he has got a job, he'll fetch her. What must she be doing till now? Would she ever realize what hazards he has to live through? If he told her she would perhaps laugh it off, or maybe she'll express mild amazement, that's all!

Where shall Niranjan keep his wife? In the same *kholi* (wretched room) where he lives? But is that a place worth living? Full of unceasing clamour and hullabullo! And the landlord's threats to cap it all, 'I have to rebuild it, so you better vacate.'

It is all rot—building anew and all that. Whenever somebody complains, he has to perform this ritual of threatening, so that he does not have to spend on repairs.

And is he able to fully use what little space he has got? Since half the roof leaks during the rains, he has to dump his baggage into a corner.

Niranjan is nervous. And lo! Yet another lorry coming... Today he had left his things scattered in the room. Water must have thoroughly drenched them.

The lorry is approaching.

Niranjan repeats to himself the curse Banshi had used for the road. With some effort he checks himself from blabbering it out. The lorry passes by. He is relieved now that the ordeal is over. He feels lighter. Nanku has finished his *laai*.

It is not raining. 'That's good,' thinks Niranjan. Then again his wife returns to his thoughts. The village is far away and here he is, driving a lorry, braving the rain and storms. When shall we meet again?

What a narrow road. It's terrible driving a lorry on it. If only to cheer himself up, he recalls that chatterbox of an old Garhwali driver in the army, who would often relate the difficulties of truck driving during the war. Aeroplanes zoom over your head, every moment parked with dangers...and soon... Startled, Niranjan looks up. No, there are no planes above. But the clouds are rumbling.

Banshi perhaps is feeling sleepy. 'Banshi, are you sleepy?'

'Who says?' a wide-eyed Banshi asks him.

'I hope both the tarpaulins are safe up there?'

'Don't you worry, Drebher Saab. They are safe.'

At the turn the road is uneven. The lorry is tilted. He is gasping and nervous. Banshi has again opened his eyes. Nanku sticks his neck out of the window.

'Chalo, Chalo,' he says.

'O God!' sighs Niranjan.

A surprised Nanku looks at Niranjan. Then, smiles. 'A green horn, that's why,' he mutters.

Niranjan is again restless. He wants to compose himself but fails. God knows how many times he will have to pass this road. He is speeding ahead with the lorry in desolation. He remembers his home, his wife.

Drizzling has again set in. No, he won't ever succeed as a driver. But then what will he do?

'I don't mind being a driver provided the roads are broad, provided they are not ridden with ditches,' he repeats to himself, with the naivety of a child. The way Banshi and Nanku have abandoned the world irks him. The way they have dozed off!

He looks up ahead intently. The rain's non-stop. He is restless. Nobody understands. And now this rain.

The wipers are licking the wind screen. But that's hardly a help. You still cannot see very far. He looks ahead intently and tries to sit firmly in his seat.

Belongings

Saamaan

She felt a pang of shock and instinctively groped for the suitcase lying nearby. No doubt they had left the table-cloth behind. She cast a frightened side-glance at Ravi who, with his head lowered, seemed immersed in contemplation. She had almost divulged her doubt when suddenly she turned to look out of the window. There were felled trees, fields, and a few scattered trees still extant as far as she could see. She began to calmly turn over everything in her mind. At the time of departure, she had gathered up all the things most carefully. She remembered she had folded up the table-cloth. There was that ever-open almirah, but now she can't recall if she had actually put the piece in the suitcase. Once again, she felt an impulse to confide in Ravi. But then, what was the use? He would be perturbed to no avail and would pester her with too many questions. Sheer irritation. During these two years of their marriage, she had realized that Ravi was given to anxiety over small things. Of course, she also knew by now why he was so irritable. A loss of anything, even a tooth-brush, meant expenditure all anew, disorder hard to control. By and by, she had learnt not to take offence at his persistent questions.

The bus came to a halt and Ravi asked if she wanted water.

'No!' she replied softly, though she was a little thirsty. Her mind was filled with an uneasiness and she wanted to be left alone for a while. She ran her eyes over the scene outside: Petty shops of grain or cloth; people lying on cots over the platforms. Through the windows and doors above the shops, she noticed a few human faces, busy in their daily chores. Amidst the ever-flowing dust and din of the buses and lorries these people go on living at this place! The thought again shook her up. A lorry shot past their bus and she turned inwards.

She had brought the tooth paste and brush... perhaps she had also kept the table cloth... No, it was left behind. The scene of that room came alive before her mind's eye. Once again she tried to think about the table-cloth, but she could not concentrate.

She didn't know when she would again visit her younger sister. And nobody knew when someone from there would be visiting her. What a beautiful and precious table-cloth! It made the whole room look gay. And Ravi, delighted, had said on the first day, 'You deserve a reward for such an exquisite choice!'

She heaved a sigh. Nervousness was growing on her. She now thought of her two rooms where dust must have gathered during their long absence. Since yesterday itself she had been brooding over it; how would she clean the rooms and put everything in order as soon as she arrived at home. But now it seems it hardly matters whether the rooms are cleaned or not. Ravi used to say that these two things, the blue table-lamp shade and the table-cloth, were like two benevolent task-masters who could extract a lot of work from him. And she had herself noted that he sometimes really sat leaning over the table, checking answer-books, or writing something continually, late into the nights. In the winter evenings, whenever alone, she too found it pleasant to read a book leaning over the table, or even musing idly lying on the bed, or knitting.

But what remained of the room now! A resentment against Ravi began to well up. We are neither too poor, nor too rich. An ordinary lectureship. But we can't do without three or four visits a week to an expensive restaurant! And then books and magazines and papers...

'Check up the luggage,' said Ravi, softly.

She wanted to retort: What luggage is there to be checked up!

But she picked up the ruck-sack and the bag that were lying near her feet and put them on the empty seat opposite her. She put on her sandals.

'Get up!'

Ravi lifted the luggage and hired a rickshaw. The sun was harsh and the streets empty.

'I shall take a bath as soon as we are home,' Ravi said softly.

She was quiet. Still thinking about the table-cloth. She wouldn't tell Ravi anything until she had opened the suitcase and made sure.

She was terribly tired by the time they reached home. She had been quiet on the way in the rickshaw and was planning to lie down on her bed and try to relax. She would cover her face with the pillow, and should Ravi dare say anything about the lost table-cloth, she would still keep her mouth shut.

She opened the door as they reached home. She sat down on the bed, waiting for Ravi to go in for his bath so that she could open the suitcase and look for the table-cloth. After a while, Ravi started fumbling for something in the bag.

'What are you looking for?'

'Where have you put the soap case?'

'It was in this itself.'

'It's not here.'

She was irritated. Remember the scenes he creates before every departure! As if the world were on fire! He wants you to hurry up—who would not lose the track of things under such demands!

'Look up in the suitcase.'

'Soap in the suitcase?'

She took the bunch of keys and opened the suitcase. This way she would also find out about the table-cloth. Nervously, she took out clothes one after the other from the suitcase. There was no trace of the table-cloth! Nor the soap-case.

'It is not here. Wait! There was a soap in the almirah,' she said as she opened the almirah and took out a cake of soap and handed it to Ravi. He made for the bathroom.

She closed the almirah and lay down on the bed. She was trying to console herself. Ravi will get a little mad at her, that's all, and then they will go buy some cloth and she will embroider it. But, her nervousness persisted.

The table lay near the bedstead and it looked strange without the table-cloth. The room, too, looked desolate and disheveled in the semi-darkness.

Ravi was asking her, 'Won't you take a bath?'

'I will,' she said slowly. 'The table-cloth is missing.' She wanted to add that she had advised him against carrying it there, for he wasn't going to read or write there, and in any case, can you in decency fold up and wrap something after having spread it out at somebody else's table? 'I have to read and write wherever I am,' Ravi had said.

She looked at Ravi in anticipation.

'Nothing to beat it!' said Ravi, and picked up a small mirror from the almirah and began peering into it after parting his hair.

She remembered, as she noticed the mirror in Ravi's hand, how a large beautiful mirror hanging on the wall had been shattered only about a month ago—all due to a slight carelessness on her part. You could keep the comb, powder, etc., in the drawers of the mirror. And how convenient it was! Now the comb lies here and the mirror there. Recalling the loss and Ravi's wrath, she noticed that Ravi this time did not lose his temper! Perhaps he is immensely satisfied with this trip!

'We shall write them to send us the table-cloth.'

'No, no! What is the hurry! When someone comes from there, he'll bring it along,' Ravi said. A great burden seemed to have been removed from her head!

'Take a quick bath and then we shall have tea.'

'Just a minute!' she intoned and got up and walked off towards the bathroom.

The bath refreshed and lightened her mind. Yet she was again reminded of the table-cloth and soap-case as she laid the soap on the table.

She usually avoided tea in a sultry weather, but today she was quite keen on it. She made tea swiftly, and after giving a cup to Ravi, she also began to sip from the cup she had poured herself.

She scanned the room as she sipped her tea. The suitcase caught her eye and gave a start. Leather at one corner of it was torn. So many days, and yet I haven't made a cloth-cover for it!

Throughout the bus-journey she had a feeling that she was unable to notice or hear anything. But now, she recalled every minute detail of the sojourn, and she began to think about the places she had seen on the way, dusty and disheveled! The house of her younger sister and her neighbouring houses! Her own disorderliness and privations stabbed her. She was caught in a whirl-wind of strange feelings. She began to see in her imagination all those houses and rooms filled with things, decorated.

'Is there any tea left?'

She almost started as Ravi asked this, and saying yes, she took the cup from him.

'One of these days we will go and buy cloth for the table. It doesn't look nice without a cover.'

'Why some day—today itself! If the other one is returned by them, we'll have two instead of one. We can wash and change them, then!'

Ravi added with a smile: 'It's rather well that we left the table-cloth there. You didn't give your younger sister anything at all for a present!'

'We should also get a mirror,' she said.

'Oh yes!' said Ravi, putting the cup down and closing his eyes.

Surveying the room in the dim light, she was again lost in the thought of such little belongings that can revive and beautify a dull and dreary existence. Her own, as well as that of the others. If only one could do away with the petty privations!

Acknowledgements

My profuse thanks to the editors and publishers who in their journals, magazines and newspapers have published these stories first, and sometimes for the second or third time over the decades:

Debonair, The Patriot Magazine, The Times of India, Indian Express, Indian Literature, Around and *The New Quest.*

I am particularly grateful to Mahendra Bhalla who had sort of vetted my translation of 'Doggery'. I also thank my wife Chandra Kiran Rathi for helping me finalize the drafts of 'The House' and 'The Beginning'. These two translations were first published under her name, for some peculiar reasons.

